HARD

KNOCKS

U

FOR LITERARY HEAT

WARNING: This book is for sale to **ADULT AUDIENCES ONLY**. Contains graphic gay male sex, reluctance, anal sex, devious logic, possible non consent, sex toys, and multiple partners all of which may be considered offensive by some readers.

All sexually active characters in this work are at least 18 years of age.

HARD

KNOCKS

U

BY

HABU

CONTENTS

CHAPTER ONE: ALL VERY LOGICAL

It was the first month at my university, where I'd transferred from a junior college for my junior year at a larger institution. University life was a whole lot different from junior college. High school—and even junior college—was a pretty small fishbowl in comparison, and I was feeling a little lost on this big college campus. In high school I ran with both the brainy kids and the jocks, and was accepted by both. I had lots of friends and I could always count on being the best, or near best at everything, and to be popular. I was on the top of the world. Junior college was in the same town as my high school. People knew and remembered me. I just kept on building on being somebody.

Coming to the university was starting all over again. It was proving I was a person—and had talents and abilities—all over again, and I wasn't doing too well at that. I wasn't the brilliant sports standout I'd thought I was back at that Podunk high school.

I was determined that, if I was going to excel in nothing else here at the university, it was going to be in academics. So, I put my nose to the grindstone on that. What suffered, though, was taking the time and effort to figure out this new university lifestyle world. It certainly wasn't anything like I'd known before.

But academics was the choice, and it was my turn today for the "introductory" evening with my logic professor, Paul Hollings. It was important that I made a good impression on the professors. They were going to be my rock in becoming somebody here. When I'd asked someone who'd taken his class the previous year what the proper attire for such a one-on-one event with a professor was, he had just given me a lopsided grin and said, "For a handsome guy like you? I'd suggest very bulky clothes."

He hadn't elaborated, but I probably should have caught on just from that comment.

It was more than an hour after dinner and the professor and I were sitting together in wingback chairs, almost knee to knee, before an enticing fire in a mammoth fireplace, complete with white bearskin rug in front of it, and our second snifter of brandy, when Professor Hollings brought the discussion around to the topic of his course, logic.

"You asked me for the short explanation of this course we're embarking on together, Ron. Perhaps the best way I can explain how logic works is by a little role play. Are you game for that?" He looked oh so charming and enthusiastic about his topic as he sat there looking deeply into my eyes. He probably was more than twenty years older than I was, but I had no doubt that the women in his classes swooned over his classic good looks and his charisma. I bet he wove quite a spell over his students in his classroom.

"Umm, yes, of course," I answered blithely and without a clue to what lay ahead.

"Okay, now for logic to really work, we have to be completely honest and open in our statements. Are you okay with that?"

"Well, sure, of course."

"All right. Now we'll have to pick a topic. Let's see, what is uppermost on a university student's mind?"

"Getting good grades that lead to a good job?" I offered.

"No, no, those are noble thoughts, but you aren't really being honest now, are you? Look, you're a young, good looking, healthy guy. What is it you really are thinking of the most?"

I just smiled.

"Come on. This won't work if you don't follow the rules of open honesty."

"Okay, okay," I responded. "Sex, of course."

"Bingo. Sex. And what is it about sex that you think of?"

I thought for a few minutes and then answered, "Getting it. The pleasure of it; the feeling it gives, which is like nothing else we experience."

"Very good, now, see, it wasn't hard to be open and honest about that, was it?"

And with that, he leaned in toward me and put both of his hands on my thighs, just above the knees. I flinched and scooted back a bit into the wingchair.

"This is just a role play, Ron. I have done this to make a point in logic. Relax. Now, what made you flinch? How did you feel when I put my hands on your thighs?"

"Nervous, trapped, a little frightened perhaps," I answered.

"Precisely. And why is that?"

"Because it was too intimate. It is wrong," I answered.

"Ah, now, that's the crux of it, where logic has to be considered," Hollings said with a laugh. And he moved his hands a bit farther up on my thighs, which made me flinch again.

"There, see, you have conditioned yourself," Hollings said. "Let's examine the logic of this. First, are you married?"

"No."

"Do you have a significant other?"

"No, not really. Not right now."

"Are you clean? No communicable diseases?"

"Excuse me!" I responded, in shock.

"Bear with me. This is just for the purposes of a logical construct."

"Well, no, of course not. Not any diseases, I mean."

"Can I assume you are over eighteen? Your transcripts indicate you are a junior college transfer."

"Yes, I'm nineteen," answered. "But what does that . . . ?"

"I thought so, but you look so young. When you think of sex and the pleasure you get from that, do you think that this is wrong for you to do? An open and honest answer now."

"No . . . no, I suppose not."

"And if you aren't hurting anyone else, if there's no one else, no one at all, who would be hurt by your gain of pleasure, would you be wrong to enjoy that pleasure?"

"Uh, no, I guess not."

"And honestly, Ron, can you openly and honestly say that you aren't gaining pleasure from me having my hands where they are?"

"Ummmm."

"Openly and honestly now, Ron. I'm sitting here right in front of you, and I can tell just by looking at your lap that you are gaining pleasure from this."

And it was true, I'm sorry to say. My body was betraying the pleasure I felt at his touch. I don't know if it was the brandy or the fire or his charisma and good looks or how he had logically gotten from there to here, but I was definitely being drawn under his spell. It didn't for a minute occur to me that he was in a position of authority and I was trying oh so hard to leave a favorable impression—to have him pleased with me.

"Here, let me move my hand here, just for logic's sake, and you tell me openly and honestly that this does not give you pleasure." He moved his right hand to my basket and had it laying lightly along the length of my cock, which was rising under the fabric of my pants.

I couldn't respond verbally immediately. My body was providing my open, honest response. But I eventually managed to croak out, "But I'm not gay. It's not right for me—"

"Ah, let's keep this based in logic, Ron. You have no obligations to anyone else; you have no health considerations that would give you obligations to any sex partner you might have; we've agreed that, like any healthy person your age, you are focused on personal pleasure and sex. You are of age to make your own choices. So, for the purposes of this role playing of ours, by what logic would you be inhibited to take your pleasure from anywhere you found it? You have grown up. You are at a major university school now, the center of learning without limits. Is it logical to be bound by any taboos of society under these circumstances?"

"Noooo, I suppose not. But—"

"Here, in terms of role playing this construct of logic we are exploring, let's see whether this increases or decreases your pleasure." His right hand went to the buttons of my shirt and then slipped into the opening and ran lightly around my chest, finding a nipple and nesting there. With his left hand, he undid my belt buckle, unbuttoned the fastening there, slowly pulled down my zipper, and placed his hand over my cock, through my briefs. I was breathing pretty heavily now.

"Ah, I can see—and feel—that you are having pleasure. There, see what logic can clear away." His left hand came up to my belly, which had now been exposed by his other wandering hand and then back under the waistband of the briefs and cupped my balls and wrapped its fingers around the base of my cock.

I tried to rise, but was only pushing my cock into his grasp.

"Uh, Professor Hollings, I don't think . . . I don't want—"

"What? You don't want to have pleasure? Pleasure that won't hurt anyone else?"

"No. I mean, I don't—"

"You don't want to have harmless sex? You want to deny yourself harmless pleasure? Where's the logic in that?"

"That's not what—"

"And me. You don't want to please me? One of your professors, who you will face this whole semester? When there's only harmless pleasure for both of us? Logic. Think logically now."

Bingo. He'd hit me where I was most vulnerable.

He had my cock out in the open now, and he was stroking it and running his hand all over it, and squeezing it, and all of my attention now was focused on my cock, the sexual pleasure I was receiving there.

"There is no one else to know what we do here this evening, Ron. You are entirely free to try new experiences, to explore what else there is out there in the world that you might enjoy but haven't tried yet. I am only trying to help you learn here, to experience all that people go to university to test out. Don't tell me you haven't thought of experiences like this before—been tempted to try them out. You're too intelligent—and too young and good looking—not to have done so. I can be your friend here at the university. It's quite useful to have professors as friends. You are smart enough to know that."

And then I thought, what the hell. What's the use of fighting logic, and I just relaxed back into the chair.

Hollings sensed that I had given in and that now he was completely in command. He brought his mouth down to

14

my lap and took my cock in, holding it firmly at the base and squeezing, while his tongue ran over and around my glans, and taking my cock into his mouth and twisting it around inside, swallowing to the root and then slowly pulling out. In, out, in out, until he could sense that I was ready to explode. Then his mouth came off and I felt a cloth over my glans, and he pumped me with his hand until I spewed cum into the cloth. It was somewhat disconcerting to realize that he had the presence of mind to be concerned about his furniture at a time like this.

"There, did that give you pleasure?"

"Yes. But—"

"And do you feel you have hurt anyone else by taking that pleasure?"

"No . . . I suppose not."

"Very good. Right answer. Now stand up and face me." I did so, and he pulled my unbuttoned shirt off my back. "Very nice, he said. You are in great shape. You must find time to work out a lot."

"Not a lot, but I make time, yes."

"Look at those nice, taut nipples." He squeezed and pinched them both, and I flinched. But this time he didn't have to ask me if I felt pleasure.

"Well-defined pecs and such a nice six pack. Ah, to be young again." He ran his hands down the side of my torso and underneath the waistband of my pants and underwear and stripped them down and off me; then went the shoes and socks.

"There, that's how God made us to be. Oh, and I see that you're revving up again. Yet again, the rewards of youth and good conditioning. What is that completely hard? seven, eight inches?"

"How would I know? I don't go around measuring myself."

"Oh, please. Open and honest now. I know you've taken measurements and compared. Don't be coy."

"Umm, about seven and a quarter, I guess."

"Thought so. I certainly can't compare, but let's see how you think I've weathered. Remember now, I have almost three decades on you." With that, he stepped back, and pulled his turtleneck sweater over his head. Not bad for someone around fifty, I had to admit. He was a redhead and his chest was thinly covered with fuzzy curls that looked a shade or two redder than the hair on his head, which had some gray shot through it. He was lean and wiry, but firm. Off came his pants and red briefs and there he stood, with a half hard-on, which was about the normal size I'd seen around the locker rooms, but was highlighted by extending out of a flaming bush of pubic hair. He had runner's legs, sinewy but lean. He threw his arms out wide.

"There. Does that give you any pleasure?"

"Well, umm."

"I know. I'll bet you are more a touch than a visual man. Here take my hands."

I extended my arms out to meet his extended hands, and he grasped my hands in his in a powerful grip. Then he walked right into me.

"There. Close your eyes. Let your senses go to where we touch. Feel our chests and nipples touching, Feel your belly against mine. There, I feel your belly quivering. Feel your pubic hair interlacing with mine. And there, as I lean into you, feel your penis rubbing mine. Here, as I rotate my hips against yours, do you feel the sensual sensations? Does this give you pleasure?"

"Yes," I whispered.

"Yes, yes. I know you're being honest. I can feel you hardening again. While I think I need to stop this for a while and rest. Oh, to be your age again. Before you open your eyes, though, just one more sensual connection." He put his lips on mine and I flinched away.

He laughed. "Think of what we're doing, what else is touching here. Do you think you'll be ruined by touching here too? That you'll never be able to do it with one of your girlfriends now? Logic. What is the logic here?" He put his lips on mine again, and this time I opened to him and found that a man's kiss could be as sweet as a woman's.

"Now, open your eyes and look over at the fire. Doesn't that look inviting?"

"Yes."

"Doesn't that bearskin rug look silky and soft and inviting as well?"

"Yes."

"Now, I want you to go over and lay down on that rug, and I'll show you the pleasure that a good back massage can give."

I went over and laid down on the rug on my belly, parallel to the fireplace. He came down beside me and started rubbing my back and shoulders with a cooling ointment.

"Now, while I'm rubbing you, connect with the rug." he said. "See what sensual pleasure you can get from the soft, silky bear's pelt." I did as he directed and found the sensations of the thick hair and the warming fire beside me to be very pleasurable.

"Move on the rug," he said, "Work your way into the nap."

I wasn't sure what he was asking, but I dug my forearms into the rug and moved my chest around. The sensation of the bear hair on my chest and nipples and belly, combined with his rubbing of ointment on my back, was titillating, and I found myself sighing with pleasure. I could feel him straddling me now, astride my buttocks; his cock nestled in the crack there. He was working on my lower back with the ointment and the rub, and he was moving his pelvis back and forth, with his cock running back and forth in my crack and up onto the small of my back. Then he slid farther back on me, straddling my thighs, his cock now between my thighs, continuing what had to be acknowledged was a dry humping of me in my inner thighs. I wasn't at all sure I liked that he was doing this, but I was trapped by his charisma and his hold of authority and, by my own pleasure in the feel of the rug and the ointment on my back—and, yes, even the movement of his cock in the recesses of my body. He started rubbing the ointment into my butt cheeks.

"What a nice bubble butt you have, he said. It must drive the women wild."

Well, yes, I had heard that on more than one intimate occasion. He must have spilled the ointment, because I felt it running across my butt and into my crack. He went after it with long slender fingers, and I jerked and flinched as he ran a finger across my asshole, but not being able to prevent a large portion from pooling there and seeping in.

This attention had fully engorged me, and I felt pinched with my cock smashed between the rug and my body. The professor started to help in that area, though. His circular motions, as he rubbed the ointment into my butt, caused my pelvis to move around on the bearskin rug, and I found myself falling into a natural gyrating humping motion. I had barely realized that I was fucking the bearskin rug, when the professor spoke.

"There, that's right. Feel the sensation. Somewhere in the hair of this rug, there's the entrance to paradise, the nicest cunt you've ever known." He took my hips in his hands and helped me rotate and hump against the rug. I was panting and moaning, and I could feel the quiver in his hands as they gripped and rotated my hips. I gave a cry as I shot off, into the nap of the bear rug, and collapsed. The professor stopped his rotation of my hips and even his own dry humping in my thighs and held me very still for a moment.

"As sensual as that was," he said at length from above my back in a husky voice, "There are sensations of pleasure you have been denying yourself that I bet no woman has given you. You've come this far this evening. You're not likely to ever permit yourself the pleasures of this evening again. Let me give you an even greater pleasurable feeling. Not at all taboo; men with too much to give go to doctors all the time for this procedure. This release—and gratification. There's nothing logical about denying yourself this level of pleasure."

"I don't know," I whispered from below. "I just don't—"

"Nonsense, you are in the real world now; you are at the university. You have come here to be educated, right?"

"Right."

"And are you the one to determine what you need to know to be educated? Isn't that what your professors are for. Isn't that logical?"

"Well, I don't—"

"Here, up on your knees, No, not all the way up. You can keep your chest resting on the rug and can stretch your arms out to be comfortable. There, yes, that's right. Now you've heard about the prostate, haven't you?"

"Yes."

"And, I'm sure you heard both that it's the man's G-spot and can give more sensual pleasure than stimulation of the penis can and that some men build up so much sperm so fast that they have to go to the doctor and be milked by stimulation of the prostate, haven't you."

"Well, yes, I guess. I've read about it," I lied. This was all new to be, but I was so afraid that ignorance of it would tell him I was stupid, that I was just a nobody from Podunk high. "But, I don't know . . ." All the time he was rubbing and squeezing my butt cheeks and thighs.

"And you know where the prostate is, don't you?"

"Up my ass, I think?" I really was guessing. It seemed the only logical place it could be considering what he was doing to find it.

"That's right. Now to get there, though, we most likely will have to prepare you and open you up. Now, let's see." I felt his hands pulling my butt cheeks apart and it felt like maybe he blew on my asshole. Whatever, the ointment still pooled there got real cool all of a sudden. "Ah, yes. It's very tight. It looks like a very tight entry." There was a catch in his voice. "Here, I'll have to do some preparation." I felt his lips on my asshole, and his tongue. He was licking my ass.

"Professor, I don't. I don't think I need—"

"Experimentation, son," the professor said. "You've come to the university to experience life. Lots of men go to the doctor and pay good money for this." He held my butt cheeks firmly in place and spread apart as his mouth went back to working my ass. He was licking and slurping and rimming me with his tongue. And I couldn't help it after a couple of minutes of this. I was sighing and moaning and grinding my butt into his face, so that when his tongue went in, I was willing it to come in farther. He stopped and laughed, slapped my butt cheek, and reached up with a hand and encased my again engorging cock.

"There, I can tell you like this. God, to have your stamina; tell me this is giving you pleasure."

"Yes," I groaned.

"Do you want me to stop?"

"No," I groaned.

"Come again? Do you want me to stop?"

"No, no, don't stop," I said in a louder voice.

"Want to know . . . want to feel what all this G-spot prostate experience is about now?"

"Yes . . . I guess so."

"You are quaking. Why are you quaking?"

"I guess I'm scared. I'm scared of what is happening."

22

"Ah, welcome to the university—forever penetrating the unknown. But trust me; you can trust me."

And with that, I felt another large glop of the ointment drop between my crack and he was working it into my ass with his fingers, fingers that were probing ever deeper into my ass.

"Uh, your fingers. Your fingers are . . . uhhh!"

"That's what I have to use to get to your prostate. There are, of course, other methods, but we are working on the medical one now, so tight. Come on, just relax. Ah, there we go; now we're there."

I jerked and lurched as my body betrayed me. Something inside my ass had actually grabbed his finger and drawn it in, and then I felt the oddest, most sensual sensation. The pad of his finger had landed on what must have been my prostate, and it rubbed that gland gently but relentlessly. I writhed and moaned and groaned under him. Electric sensations went through my body, and I felt, at first, like I had to piss, and then cum started dribbling out of my cock, and it I'd had time to reload, I'm sure I would have ejaculated again.

But then the finger was gone, to be replaced by something thicker than the finger, and I realized that he had entered me with his cock. I was being fucked by my professor. I protested loudly.

"No, No. Get off—"

"This is about pleasure, pleasure that doesn't hurt anyone else," the professor answered me amid his heavy

23

breathing. "It's about my pleasure as well as yours. And it's about your education, your experiencing everything before deciding what you want to do, what path you want to follow. What's the logic to denying any possibility without knowing what you're denying? Answer me that son. What's the logic in that?"

But I didn't need to answer, because almost as quickly as he had begun, he had finished. When he realized he was about to climax, he pulled out of me and came across the small of my back in one fairly weak eruption. He cleaned my back with his cloth and let me collapse onto the bearskin rug.

"There, and that is why you'd want to take logic, son. With logic you can talk your way into anything you want to do. This little role play illustrated that point quite nicely, I think. I'm going to go take a shower now. You can see your own way out. And I'll be looking forward to seeing you in class. A good job; a very nice body and a tight ass. I think you are going to do very well this semester." And he was gone.

After a few minutes, I stood up, nursing a few stabbing pains and a soreness inside me that I'd never felt before, bleakly pulled on my clothes, and went out into the night. I hadn't been this far away from home and at the university for more than a week. What a chump.

But I'd also gotten at least one professor to know who I was and to like me and know me well—if maybe he didn't know me well in quite the way I had planned. I blushed at the

24

thought of his hands all over my naked body—and his mouth on my cock and of him inside me. Yes, indeed, he knew me real well.

He had made it sound so logical every fucking step of the way. It was like shooting fish in a barrel. I was just a country yokel on this campus. But what was done was done—and I didn't have to do it again if I didn't want to. I wouldn't be this dumb again if something like this got started. And, right now, I felt like I'd be sore inside forever and I'd always have that to remind me of what I didn't have to fall for ever gain—if I didn't want to.

CHAPTER TWO: A COLLEGE DORM IS NOT SANCTUARY

I trudged back to the dorm from having, dumb me, been easily seduced by my logic professor—even after the very clear warning I'd gotten. I was feeling very down and very sore, hoping that no one would ever learn about my humiliation. I was angry at the professor, not knowing how I was going to be able to sit in his class in front of him now. And, the more I thought about it, the more I was worried about whether and what demands he might make on me for the rest of the semester. I wasn't that way. I didn't want to be that way. Nothing like this had ever happened to me in my safe world—my world before coming across country to this university.

When I reached my dorm room, I didn't even turn on the light. My roommate, Lance, was already asleep in his bed. Or, so it seemed. His covers were rustling, so maybe he was jacking off again. He was always jacking off and always so proud to show off his dick. Granted it was a long one, maybe eight inches, but it was thin and had a crook to the side near the end. He said that just made it all the more enjoyable for his partners.

I wouldn't know. I wasn't one of his partners.

Under the circumstances, I just felt disgusted and bummed out. And I felt I had to wash the filth of my experience this evening off my body—especially because the professor was right, I had enjoyed it and it was logical that I shouldn't feel any guilt over enjoying it. I hadn't hurt anyone else while receiving considerable pleasure. I grabbed a towel off my rack in the dark and my soap from the basin, stripped down, and headed for the shower. It was 1:00 a.m., but steam was pouring out of the communal shower when I arrived. I turned to leave, not wanting to see anyone just now, but a voice boomed from the depths of the shower.

"Who's that? Someone there?"

I recognized the voice of the dorm counselor, Nate, a wrestling scholarship student in his last year of eligibility. He had been real nice in greeting me when I had arrived at campus, my car filled to the brim from the cross-country drive, already lonesome for home. Strange he was using the

28

communal shower, however; I thought he had a bathroom of his own in the counselor's apartment.

"That you, Nate?" I called out. "It's kinda late for a shower, isn't it."

"Late wrestling practice tonight; trying to get the knots out, but yes, it's late for a shower. What's your excuse?"

"A late dinner at a professor's," I answered, as I tossed my towel on the bench and entered the steam. I could barely make him out on the other side of the shower room, a big, black monster of a man, with bulging muscles everywhere— everywhere but downstairs, though, I could see. His penis, obviously in repose, barely peeked out of his black bush of pubic hair. What was showing, though, showed an extra large, cut head.

"At the professor's? What professor?" he called out to me. He was vigorously scrubbing away under his arms and across his massive chest with a sponge.

"Uhh. Professor Hollings, the logic professor."

A brief pause, and then a snort, "I see."

I wondered what he "saw." I harkened back to the warning I got before I went to Professor Hollings' house, and I reddened up, as I soaped up, wondering just how many people knew about Professor Hollings and his "meetings" with his new students.

I heard the sound of something hitting the floor of the shower and skidding past me into the corner. I looked up, and

29

Nate was standing closer to me, a little smirk on his face. I couldn't help but notice that he was stirring down below. Not long, by any means, but bigger now, much bigger around, and sticking out farther.

"Soap, I dropped my soap," he said with a grin. "It's there behind you. Can you reach it for me?"

"Sure, Nate," I said and I turned and bent over—and he was on me in a flash. He had his big mitts wrapped around the front of my thighs and was diving for my asshole with his tongue.

"No, Nate, stop that!"

"Ah, I smell the professor's ointment and his scent. He's been up here, hasn't he?"

"Nate! God, get off me!"

"Scream all you like, Pretty Boy. Everyone on this hall knows I take what I want when I want it. Hollings has been in you, hasn't he? He's been fucking you, hasn't he?"

I tried to pull away, tearing at his hands, but he moved one of his hands between my legs and grabbed my balls and squeezed. I screamed in pain.

"Stop squirming or I'll castrate you, right here and now. Gave you that lecture on logic and pleasure, didn't he? And then couldn't hold himself; came almost as soon as he got it in you, didn't he?"

"Nate, no. Yes, yes, he seduced me. What do you want me to say. And I'm here to clean him off me. I don't—"

"Well, tonight you do. I don't care about it being seconds. I've had my eye on you since you rolled in here. Come on, open up again, Baby. Ah, that's better."

A guy from down the hall, Tim, I think is name was, came into the shower room, just a towel around his midsection. He looked surprised. I looked up and gave him a "get me out of this" look.

"Uh, I thought."

"I know what you thought," Nate answered gruffly, his voice thick and hoarse. "I'll fuck you later. Got me a new hole to fill right now."

Tim backed out of the shower room.

Nate resumed his attack on my hole. He had his tongue in me farther than I thought a tongue could go. And he was working my balls and cock with one of his hands. He left doing that, picked up his soap from the floor, and began soaping up my ass, exchanging his tongue with his fingers. I was huffing and puffing and doing a little screaming, but he paid me no mind whatsoever. I once tried to stand back up, and he slapped me on the butt and told me to stay bent over. Then he just took one big mitt and wrapped it around my belly. He used his other hand to help guide his huge knob of a dick to my asshole, and then he just pushed his way in a couple of inches. I screamed and writhed.

"Com'on. You opened for that old professor. Open up for me. God, you've got a tight butt. The professor was the first, wasn't he?"

"Yes," I whimpered, hoping that he'd have some mercy on me.

"Argh," he yelled, as he grabbed my hips with both of his hands, and knocked my legs farther apart with one of his feet. I slipped on the filmy floor, and grabbed for the floor with my hands to keep myself from falling. I needn't have bothered. He had me well under control with his beefy hands wrapped around my pelvis on each side, his thumbs pulling my butt cheeks away from my hole.

With another "Argh," he was in another two inches, and I was being split, my ass canal opening to him whether it wanted to or not. And then he just rocked me like a rag doll, his thick dick coming a bit out when I was rocked in one direction and then a bit farther in than before when he rocked back.

"No, no," I was whimpering, but he wasn't paying a bit of attention to me. He continued with this for several minutes, obviously much better at controlling himself than the professor had done. But the steamy water was still on, and it was scalding us. So he just frog marched me out of the shower room into the main bath—without losing his position up my ass, which was quite a feat, considering his cock wasn't all that long. There was a dining-height table up against the wall to the left of the entrance of the shower room, where we all threw our wet towels to go to the laundry. With a sweep of his hand, Nate, sent the accumulated towels onto the floor and slammed me down on the surface of the table on my left side. At the same time he lifted my right leg with his left hand. He was side splitting me now, going to town with his pelvis, pumping me as vigorously as a seasoned wrestler could do. With his right hand, he was roaming my pecs and nipples, abs and stomach, cock and balls. After a couple of minutes of this position, he rotated me up to where my tailbone was barely gripping the edge of the table and my back was arched against the back wall. He held my legs out in a wishbone and continued pumping until I heard a big intake of breath and he pulled his dick out of my ass and shot his load on my stomach.

"Okay, now that was good. Really a nice piece of ass," he said, with a big grin as if we'd both had a good time, "Back to the showers."

I cowered in my corner of the shower until he had washed himself off and left the shower and main bathroom, whistling a jaunty tune. And then I scrubbed and scrubbed and scrubbed myself and dragged my wounded body back to my room.

The lights were still out, and Lance was quiet on his side of the room when I returned from the episode with Nate in the shower. Lance was a snorer, and he wasn't snoring now, so chances were good that he was awake—that he'd heard at least some of what went on in the shower room. I was so embarrassed and dejected that I just got in my bed naked, pulled the covers over me, turned my face to the wall, and cried as quietly as I could—not just from the pain in my ass, but from the humiliation of my introduction into university life.

I felt a touch on my arm, and someone sinking down onto my bed behind my thighs.

"Tough night?" Lance asked in a concerned and gentle tone.

"Yeah, I guess you could say that," I responded in a hurt voice.

"Hollings and Nate both?"

Silence and then. "Yeah. Both."

"First time?"

"Yeah. Never before."

"So, it must hurt a bit, I guess."

"Yes."

"Here, I have some ointment that will help that. Sorry, but it's the best help I can give."

A few moments of silence and then, "Okay, yeah . . . thanks."

The covers were pulled off me, and I felt cool ointment being applied to my ass.

With his other hand, Lance was gently massaging my back. After a while, Lance stretched out behind me, my butt cupped into his belly. His left arm came around me and stroked my chest. He was naked.

"Lance . . . please don't," I started.

"Shush, shush, it doesn't have to be the way you've already gotten it tonight. It can be gentle and soothing." I felt his long, thin cock between my thighs.

"Lance . . ."

He moved up on me, and the tip of his cock was against my asshole and then, ever so slowly and for such a long time, it just glided into me and up my ass canal, farther, ever so farther than either Hollings or Nate had reached.

"Lance . . . No, no," I groaned.

He nibbled my ear and whispered into it, "Give us a kiss." His hand had already found my cock and he was stroking it. I turned my head and we went into a long kiss. Sometime in the middle of that, he began to slowly pump me, sending shivers throughout my body.

Our kiss was broken, and I whispered, "Lance, Lance . . . yes, yes, oh yes." At length we had both come, and I drifted off to sleep, still wondering how I had gotten into this position, Lance snoring behind me, his arm thrown across my torso, his crotch nestled into my butt, and his long, slender, now-soft dick up to the root in my ass.

CHAPTER THREE: SOMETIMES A COLLEGE DEAN ISN'T SANCTUARY EITHER

I had been sexually assaulted by three men within my first week at school. Nothing like this had ever happened to me before. I let it go for several days and then, when I was on my way to throw some hoops at the gym, I just snapped and found myself seeking out the dean of men students. I didn't know if I could get a walk-in appointment with him, but I felt like I needed to talk to someone about what was happening to me.

I walked into his outer office and encountered another student at the secretary's desk—a well-built blond guy, who gave me a smile that made me think that even he knew what I'd been doing—or, rather, what had been done to me—this past week. When I asked if I could see the dean, he asked me my name and said that I was in luck, that the dean had just come back from a practice. I remembered then that the dean was also the university's wrestling coach. And, from the looks of his secretary when he got up and escorted me to the door, he was probably on the team as well, at some middleweight level.

I also remembered that I intended to search the coach out anyway, as I was interested in joining the wrestling team. I just hadn't let myself think about that until I had the academics in control.

I entered the office. Dean Seeman was a big, burly guy with heavy muscles rather than fat. He was still in his gym clothes, gym shorts, and a loose T-shirt with a deep scoop at the neck and both of the armholes. He was a real bear, black curly hair everywhere.

When we entered the office, the secretary announced my name, and even before I could say anything about why I was here, the dean pushed his chair out from the desk and waved me over with a beefy mitt.

"Oh yeah. I've been hearing about you. Hollings send you over for my lunch snack? Good man, Hollings." He grabbed me by the hips and turned me this way and that way.

"Uh, no, Dean. It's about Professor Hollings, but he didn't—"

"Said you were a good lay. Said you had a great butt—" He pulled my shorts down off my butt cheeks and squeezed them and gave them a good slap. ". . . and a nice tight hole too. He said you had a sweet ass." He had a big finger working at my asshole.

"Hey . . . Ouch!" I cried.

"And Nate said you were a good screw, too, that you liked it a little rough."

Nate? He was talking to the dean—to the wrestling coach—about what he'd done to me? Of course. He was a star wrestler at this university.

"Oh Gawd, no," I cried. "I didn't come in here for this!"

"Greg, lock the door and come back and help me with this dude," the dean said to his secretary. "You can strip on the way back, but make it snappy."

I flailed around, trying to break free, but he was a wrestling coach. Probably had been a star wrestler in his day. There didn't seem to be a thing I could do about it.

"Come on now, don't pretend you don't want it," the dean was saying in a jovial voice. "Both Hollings and Nate said you panted for it. Said you were a bit of a tease too. I kinda like that."

A now-naked Greg got behind me, between me and the desk, stripped my T-shirt up and off me, and put me in a bear hug that had my arms raised over my head and his naked body behind mine. I could feel his cock rising to the occasion at the small of my back. But most of my troubles were in front of me. The dean was sitting in his chair facing me, and while Greg was stripping my T up, Seeman was pulling my gym shorts and jock down and off me. He reached around me and took a tube of ointment from a drawer and got a gob into his hand. He cupped one hand around my balls and the base of my cock.

His mouth went to my cock, and his other hand, with a big gob of ointment, went straight under my balls and up to attacking my asshole. I tried to make my legs work, to use them to break free and get out of there, but Greg got his calves wrapped around mine and held me there, like a bow, with my cock out front, being pumped by Seeman.

I would have done some loud complaining, but I was too busy moaning and groaning at what the dean was doing with my cock—and with those fingers at my asshole.

In just a few minutes, Seeman let loose of my cock, stood up, and shucked his shorts and T off. He was gigantic in every way. He stood there in front of me, working his cock and covering it with the ointment, making it huge and thick and slick. When he was satisfied, he sat back into his chair, pulled himself up to me, and grabbed me by the thighs. Greg let loose of me then, and I struggled as best I could, but Seeman just set me down astride his lap, facing him. Our cocks were rising together between us, his larger and thicker than mine. Seeman wrapped one hand around them both and started stroking them together. The other hand, covered with ointment, was back to pushing at and up my ass. All three of us were breathing heavy now, with no telling who was or was not sighing and moaning and groaning.

I came in three jerky ejaculations, which seemed to be the signal Seeman was looking for, because he released our cocks and stood back, letting Greg hold me prisoner there.

I nearly hyperventilated as I watched him open a drawer, take a stack of condom packets out, open one, and roll the condom on his cock. All the time he was leering at me and telling me how good he was going to be to me.

All I could do was whimper and beg. He chose to interpret my begging as asking for his cock. Crowned now, he leaned in to me, took me by the hips, raised them, and pulled me in toward him.

I fruitlessly cursed and pleaded, as he released my hip on one side but only so that he could guide his dick to my hole. And then he just skewered me, split me with that big sausage of his, and pulled me slowly, but steadily down into his lap until my butt cheeks felt his curly pubic hair.

"Lift him up, Greg. About six inches should do it." Greg was quick to respond; he moved his arm lock to under my pecs and lifted me up several inches. Seeman held me in place with his big mitts around my waist, just above my hips, and he started to fuck up into me, to pump me from below. Long strokes that had him pulling down so that the knob on his huge sausage was just inside my sphincter and then dragging up my prostate the full length and as far into me as he could go. I was gasping and quivering and holding my legs out as far as they would stretch to open my canal up to him as much as possible. And he pumped me for almost forever. Greg was shivering behind me, leaning back on the desk, giving himself room to dry fuck the small of my back. Seeman came inside me with several flinches and ejaculations, and, almost immediately, his cock began to soften. But he didn't withdraw it.

I went limp. It was out of exhaustion and the effect of too much frustration for too long. Seeman seemed to take it as acceptance that I wanted what was happening. He even said, "Finished teasing now, are you?" and smiled at me.

He'd fucked me now, though, so there was something of an attitude of "what's done is done" in my relaxing my body. Then, when I felt like I was going to be able to endure this, Seeman pushed me back into his lap, tipped me forward, and wrapped his big arms around my back. My face was buried in the deep, hairy sweaty crevice between his pecs; my cheeks were being gouged by the chains of a heavy gold necklace.

"Now, you too, Greg," I heard.

You too, what, Greg? I thought. But only briefly, because I felt Greg's hands on my butt cheeks and his hardened cock at my asshole, pushing in along the length of Seeman's already fully encased, if soft cock. Somehow he got in. Somehow I accommodated him.

But Seeman began to moan and grunt again as Greg's cock plowed its way up me, once again stimulating Seeman's rod, which began to harden again and to move in motion with Greg's pumps. Growing in length and thickness . . . stretching my ass canal to and beyond endurance.

"N o o o o," I screamed into Seeman's hairy chest, any noise I might have produced being muffled in his pelt there.

"Ahhhhhh!" Seeman screamed above me.

"Yessss," Greg whooped, as he withdrew his cock and came across the small of my back, followed by me coming again against Seeman's hard belly, and Seeman coming again deep, deep inside me.

I was held there, just like a rag doll, for several minutes, while Seeman and Greg kissed above me and slowly returned to steady breathing.

"Anybody ask you if you can take two cocks at once, son, the answer's yes," I heard Seeman murmur. "Kinda tight, though. We'll have to get you loosened up a bit." He gave a low laugh.

Then: "I hear the phone goin' off the hook out there, Greg. Go get it and then we'll go get us somethin' for lunch . . . in a few."

Then, as Greg padded out the door, picking up his clothes as he went, Seeman tipped me back against his desk, his once-more softened cock still buried up my ass, and I just lay there, the small of my back supported by his thighs, exhausted, defeated, my arms flopping down at my side, trying not to concentrate on my inflamed innards. Seeman lifted my legs up so they stretched up the arms of his chair, his torso between them.

"Both Hollings and Nate were right," he said, as he ran his hands up my legs, stopping to stroke my cock and balls a few times, and then on up onto my torso. "You are one nice lay. Nice balls, nice juicy cock, perky tits, really nice, tight ass." And with this, he took the base of his cock in his hand and rotated it around in my hole. My canal betrayed me by grabbing his club and contracting muscles around it. His cock began to stiffen again. His hands explored my flat belly, my abs, and my pecs.

"Great definition in these muscles," he said. "Athletic. You could be a wrestler. You should come out for wrestling. We have a tight little wrestling group. Your tight ass would be a good addition. What do you say? Come out for wrestling this semester. I could give you some one-on-one coaching."

I whimpered a nearly silent demur.

"What was that you said?" Seeman asked, his hands digging into my pecs, squeezing my nipples hard.

"Yes, coach. Yes, I'd like that."

"We could do this about every day," he said, as he took his cock again and resumed rotating it inside me. He was recovering, getting bigger. I couldn't help it; I let out a little moan.

"You like this. You're a tease, but your body don't lie. And about the wrestling and working on special holds with me after practices. Would you like that? Would you like me showing you some special wrestling moves—and being inside you, fucking your brains out nearly every day?" He had his hands on my butt cheeks, squeezing them.

"God this is a nice butt," he said. "God, you are a gift from heaven. But you don't got what I got. You want me in you every day, Stud?"

I murmured, but even I didn't know what I'd said. He stood and pushed me back down on the desk top with his pelvis, with his rising cock. He took my legs in his hands, putting them behind my knees, and wishboned my legs out. He pulled his cock out almost all of the way and then glided it back in up to the hilt.

"What was that you said? I didn't hear you. You want me to fuck you every day?" Out and then gliding back in.

"Yes, yes," I answered.

"Yes, yes, what?" Out and then in more quickly and deeper. Then he gyrated his hips, screwing his cock around in me.

"Oh God, yes, yes, I want you to fuck me." Out and then plunge and hip gyrations.

"How often. You want me to fuck you how often?" Out, in half way, out, and then dive in up to the hilt. I was panting and moaning and grunting and trying to get a hold on the edges of the desk to keep from being powered off the other side and against the wall.

"Every day. Fuck me every day, Coach."

"How hard, how deep?" He was pumping me hard now and was breathing hard, leaning into me, his left hand still holding out a leg, but the other one pumping my cock. "This deep, this hard, Coach," tears running down my face.

"Ahhhhh, Gititgititgitit," he screamed, pulling his cock out and shooting off across my belly. He came down on top of me, roughly taking my mouth in his, grabbing my wrists with his hands and pushing them over my head. After deep kissing me, his cock slipped out of my hole, and he moved his mouth down my body, licking and kissing and nibbling down my neck; into both of my pits; across my pecs, giving attention to my nipples, giving satisfied sucking and grunting noises, down my six pack, into my navel, along my heaving belly, through my pubic hair and to my cock and balls. His hands followed behind but stopped just below my rib cage, as he took my cock

46

into his mouth, and gently, but rhythmically sucked me off until I had come again.

Then he rose off me and towered over me as he pulled on his T and his shorts.

"Tell Hollings thanks for the gift, son. You were great. I don't know how long it's been since someone could get me off three times in one hour. But also tell Hollings that you'll be doing more wrestling this year than studying logic." With a laugh he had turned and swept through the door, not a care in the world, off to a late lunch with Greg. Leaving me to pick up my clothes and my life as I could and to go in search of some more of Lance's cooling ointment.

CHAPTER FOUR: FRATERNITY HAZING

It had been three days since I had been violated four times within two days, and I was hiding out. I had taken a rented-by-the-week apartment made over from a motel not too far from the campus, dropped the logic class, and kept as low a profile as I could. I'd found the former motel too noisy to study in, so I was camped out in a small overgrown park nearby, where I was studying on an old picnic table. I thought that I would be completely hidden from view, but when I sat down; I saw that I had a straight-line view of the front of one of the fraternity houses. I had been studying pretty intensely for a couple of hours, when I realized that the sound of running water was intruding into my mind. I looked over toward the fraternity house, and, to my consternation, I saw Greg, the secretary from the painful incident at the dean's office.

He had his red Thunderbird convertible out in the circular drive in front of the fraternity house, and he was washing it with a bucket of soapy water and a garden house. I tried to return to my studies, but he was mesmerizing. The events of the last week must have been getting to me, must have been working at me in some fashion. His attraction could not be denied. He was stripped down to tight, low-cut latex biker's shorts and was barefoot. It was undeniable that he had a great body and fluid motions, just what a competing wrestler needed. As he ran a sponge over the car hood and the canvas top, his muscles rippled. I watched as he stood up and pushed a blond curl back from his face. I think he must have seen me then.

He smiled invitingly, but I pretended I didn't see him. He moved around to the other side of the car and did some more sponge work, flexing his muscles and doing stretches to loosen up his back more than probably was required to be washing a car. I felt something stirring below my belt. It couldn't be. Just because I had been repeatedly fucked over the past several days couldn't mean that I responded to other men this way. But I couldn't fool myself. I had largely taken pleasure from all that had happened to me, even from the brutality of

Nate and the dean. No, I couldn't fool myself, I knew, as I put my hand in my lap and stroked myself through the silky basketball shorts I was wearing.

Greg came around to the near side of his car. He leaned over the hood and shimmied his rear end as he rubbed the sponge over the car. His butt cheeks were well defined in the biker's shorts, and they were nicely rounded. He turned full toward me, lifted the hose over his head, arched his back, and just let the water stream over his blond hair and down across his solid, well-cut torso.

I could see he was laughing. He threw the hose down; went out of sight briefly, presumably to cut off the water; and returned with a hand towel. He tossed his head back and forth to fling off the excess water and then slowly toweled himself down. He dropped the towel and languidly ran his hand over his pecs and his six pack and his belly and down to his basket. He stood stroking himself there, just as I was stroking myself where I sat, and then I saw him laugh and walk straight in my direction. I was glued to the spot by the shock that he was coming to me; I should have gotten up and hurriedly left in the other direction, but I just sat there, watching him come to me.

Greg sauntered up to the table and around to my side and leaned his butt into the edge of the table right next to me.

"Well, hello there, Stud. Do you know that lots of people have been looking for you? Professor Hollings, your roommate, Nate, even the dean—especially the dean?"

"No, I'm not really aware of that. I'm just trying to get on with my studies."

"Do you know I've been looking for you too?"

"No, why would you be looking for me?"

"I felt we didn't really get to know each other the other day. And I would really like to get to know you better. I don't even know your name. What's your name?"

"I see no reason to get to know each other better."

"You can't see why I wouldn't want to get to know you better. Here, look here." He had his hand on his basket. His cock was standing almost straight out, trying to get out of the confining tight latex. "Doesn't this explain why I'd want to get to know you better."

"It seems you already have known me better than almost anyone else," I said bitterly.

"And you want to get to know me better too, Don't you . . .? What's your name again? Could it be Peter? See, Peter is wanting to know me better." And he reached down and tweaked the tented fabric in my lap. There was no doubt that he was having an effect on me.

"I . . . I think I'd better go," I squeaked out and started to gather up my books and rise from the bench. But Greg was too fast for me. He quickly and fluidly swiveled behind me and swung his left leg around me; sitting right behind me, with me scooted up to the front edge of the bench and him barely on the back edge. I was trapped with him behind and on either side of me and the picnic table close to my chest. He wrapped his arms around me and gave a sigh. Once again, just as the other day, I could feel his insistent cock trapped between his body and the small of my back.

"Listen, Greg. I'm not really—"

"You put on quite a performance with the dean the other day. He's been downright jolly for days. Think he'd been afraid that he was moving into his Viagra years. But not after you came along."

"Look, Greg. I came to the dean to report that I'd been raped, not to turn him on. I've had no experience in—"

"Screw experience. Experience can be overrated. I like you just the way you are." He wasn't wasting time; his right hand drifted down the front of my T-shirt, went between my belly and the waistband of my shorts, found my cock, and started teasing and stroking it.

"Greg. I'm not going to—"

"Sure you are," Greg said in a steely voice. "Sure you are, but I'd much rather it was because you wanted to." With his left hand he pushed my shorts down in the back so that they were half-way down my butt cheeks, and he released his cock from his latex biker's shorts and let it run itself up the top of my butt crack and onto the small of my back. Then, with his left hand, he reached around and gently pushed my face to the side.

"Kiss me. We didn't get to kiss the other day, and it's been driving me crazy wondering how you taste."

"No, Greg, I don't do—"

"Hey, didn't Hollings give you the logic lecture? How do you know you don't want to until you've tried it? It's just logic." Then he laughed and gave me a million-dollar smile— just before his lips moved to mine. He started with a sweet lips-only kiss, but moved into a more open, deeply probing kiss. He was still stroking my cock, and I put my hand over his there, on the outer side of the material and moved with him. He was stroking up and down along my butt crack in back, dry fucking me there. He brought his hand out of my crotch and, with both hands, pulled my T-shirt up and off me and threw it to the side. His hands were flying all over my arm muscles, my pits, pecs, nipples, abs, navel, belly, and back down to stroking my cock. With a sigh, I lifted my butt a bit more, and he pulled my pants down further and continued dry fucking up my crack and onto the small of my back, this time with more cleavage to stroke in. I must admit I expected him to try to enter me again from that position, and I was marshaling my strength to try to fight him off, but before he could get around to that, he came up the small of my back in a jerk and jackoff that probably surprised him as much as me.

"See what you do to me?" he whispered in my ear while he was nibbling it. "You are delicious. The best bod I've seen on this campus in some time. I've never gotten off with just a dry fuck before."

Then he was up like a jack rabbit. "On the table. Get up there and lay down on the table."

"That's enough Greg. You got your rocks off. I've got to study."

"On the table—now!" He swept my books off the top of the picnic table, grabbed me by the elbow, and hurried me along. I lay down the length of the table, trying to be careful not to get my ass anywhere near an edge. When I was lying down, he stripped off my shorts and then his own. He had quite a formidable cock, if not either as long or thick as the coach's. All in all, he had a beautiful body, and, in spite of my misgivings, I ached for him. He knelt on the bench beside my hips and gave me suck while letting his hands roam around the rest of my body. I moaned and squirmed under his attention. Without my really realizing it, my hand sought out his cock, and I stroked him. In answer, he rose off the bench and positioned himself in a 69 position, and, for the first time in my life, I found myself kissing, licking, and sucking another man's dick.

He tasted salty and had a strong male smell, but I didn't find this unpleasant. I started to mimic doing to his cock what he was doing to mine. After a while, he moved so that I was presented with his asshole rather than his cock, and, instinctively, I did what had been done to me so many times in the last week. I moistened him up there and explored him with my lips and my tongue. He writhed above me, giving deep sighs and moans.

When I had him moistened up real well, he rose and turned and straddled me from above. With one hand holding my cock in place, he lifted his hips and then slowly came down on me, impaling his own ass with my cock. In, in I went. It was somewhat like with a woman, but it seemed tighter. He buried his hands in my chest hair, finding and working my nipples, while he slowly pumped himself. I found I was joining his rhythm, and then he lifted his hips off me a good six inches.

"You pump," he said, "you fuck me. Fuck me hard and deep."

I took over the pelvis action, sending my engorged dick up into him as far as it would go and then withdrawing half way and plunging up again. He was moaning and groaning and we both went into a wild pumping action. I had one hand wrapped around his cock now and was pumping that in rhythm to the wild tune we were playing in his ass. We came almost simultaneously. Me, pulling out of him and shooting up his belly and him shooting off up mine. He collapsed on top of me, taking my arms above my head with my wrists in his strong grasp. He kissed me long and deep and arched up a bit to permit him to kiss and nibble his way down my neck and to my nipples.

When I was truly relaxed and close to drifting off to sleep, he came off me and the picnic table top. With a laugh, he pulled his biking shorts back on.

"That was what I wanted, sport. Thanks. Don't, worry, I won't tell anyone else you are still around, hiding out. But when you want more of this, just come back to this spot to do your studying. I spared your ass this time, because I know you are still sore from the other day, but the next time, your ass is mine. And both you and I know there'll be a next time. Ciao, baby."

And he turned and strutted back to his red Thunderbird and his fraternity house, leaving me there, stretched out on the top of the picnic table, alone, and once more having been "had."

CHAPTER FIVE: TROUBLE WITH THE LAW

I'd had enough of these repeated sexual assaults; being used like this. The next day, I packed my car and headed for home. No more than three miles beyond the campus gate, though, I heard a police siren and was pulled over to the side of the road. I sat in the car, wondering what I had done wrong, as a policeman strutted around and took a look at both license plates, all the time swishing a mean-looking night stick with a short leather whip on one end. I rolled down the window as he approached. He leaned an arm on the sill and looked intently at me through very dark sunglasses.

"Let me see your license and registration, son."

"Umm, just a minute," I said, as I struggled to get the glove compartment open. "What seems to be the problem, officer?"

"License and registration please."

I handed them over to him, and he took them back to his cruiser and did some communicating into a mike on his dash. He got out of the car and sauntered back to mine. He was a tall, muscular Hispanic with an obvious attitude toward non-Hispanics.

He didn't hand my license back to me. "Now, I have to do some more checking, so I want you to pull your car up in the overgrown driveway up there. Pull in a good fifty feet. I'll be right behind you." I did as he asked. The lot obviously had been abandoned, and I don't think either my car or the cruiser could be seen from the road where we pulled to a stop. He came back to my window.

"Officer, what seems to be . . . ?"

"Step out of the car, please."

"But—"

"Get out of the car now, hands showing, and assume the position, hands out wide on top and legs apart. Farther apart and farther away from the car, now!" He tapped me—no, more than tapped me—with his nightstick on the thigh. It hurt. But I did what he said. I was put a little off balance, concentrating hard to keep my weight balanced on my hands. I figured this was probably the point.

"Got any drugs in the car?"

"Drugs? Me? No, I don't do drugs."

"That's not necessarily what your rap sheet says."

"My rap sheet? What rap sheet?"

"Got any drugs on your person?"

"Certainly not. Listen, officer—"

"Save it."

He started patting me down, doing a real thorough job, not excepting my privates. When he was finished, he stood there beside me. He seemed to be breathing a little heavy, which probably should have clued me in on what was going on here.

"Afraid I'm going to have to do a cavity search."

"Excuse me? A what?"

"Now don't go resisting an officer," he said, as he tapped me meaningfully on the cheek with the big end of his nightstick.

"Open wide," and he had his fingers in my mouth and was roughly feeling around on all sides in there.

"Now, these pants are going to have to come off."

"My pants!?"

"I said a cavity search." He tapped me on the cheek with his nightstick again, and then he put it under his arm and held my butt in his left hand as he unbuckled my belt and zipped down my pants with his right hand.

"Pull your legs together." Down and off came the pants and underpants in one movement. "Now, take the stance again." I was about ready to cry in frustration and bewilderment, but I did as he told me. His left hand was on my bare butt now, and his right was searching around my balls and cock, which was beginning to come to life.

"Can't be too careful; they're hiding it just about anywhere these days." His voice was thick, and he was breathing heavier. He got behind me, and I felt his searching fingers going for my asshole. He entered right in. I winced and turned my butt to get away from him, but he whipped me one good one with the whip on the end of his nightstick and stuck the larger end of it between my legs and into the back of my ball sack.

"Seems to me you're resisting, son. You're going to have to pay for that."

I'd had about enough of this, cop or no cop, and I began to push off the car, but quick as a flash he had two pair of handcuffs out and handcuffed me to the ends of the racks on the top of the car. Then his fingers went back to digging in my ass.

"Oh, God, no," I cried out. "Stop that! You can't—"

"I can't what, Pretty Boy?" he said close to my ear as he grabbed a handful of my hair and arched my head back. "I can do whatever I please. And you're going to let me do whatever I please." Swish, swish went the whip across my butt cheeks. And now the nightstick was being pulled back across my perineum and to my asshole and being rubbed and pushed against my asshole. All of my attention went to my asshole now and to doing all I could to open up to business end of the billy club. I was sure that he was going to fuck me with that big club and was wildly wondering if that would tear me apart so badly that I'd die. But, though he did get it pushed in an inch or two, he suddenly pulled it away.

Swish, swish. He stroked the whip end against my butt cheeks and then he slapped me on the butt a couple of times. And then I felt another rod back there, between my thighs. Not as big as the billy club, but more insistent. He pulled my T-shirt up over my head and onto my arms as far as it would go. Then he entered me from behind. Pushing pretty quickly and steadily, not really giving me enough time to open to him. I arched my back into his chest as he went in to the root, and he swished his whip across my chest and belly and thighs. Not sharp enough to cut but enough to raise welts and to cause flickers of pain. He must have had a strap with studs on it wrapped around the base of his cock, because the rim and entry of my ass were being chafed by something nobbly. He pumped me for a good fifteen minutes before he filled the head of his condom inside me, all the time slapping my butt cheeks and swishing that leather whip across my body.

And then he was all business. He pulled away from me and adjusted his uniform. He pulled my T back down onto my body. It stung where the material came into contact with the welts from the whipping. He then had me step back into my pants and he fastened me up. He took the handcuffs off me, but he forced me back into the driver seat of my car and handcuffed both of my hands to the steering wheel.

"Gotta take you in, Pretty Boy. Can't resist arrest and not be taken in for a spell."

"But, but, I didn't—"

"Drive behind me. No use trying to slip away, 'cause you can't get out of those cuffs. Just drive along behind me, like a good little piece of ass."

We drove in tandem to the police office of a small town, where it appeared that he was the only one on duty.

"Okay, back in the tank," he said, as he manhandled me out of the car, through the door of the station and toward the back room. There were four cells there, but only one occupant, a big Neanderthal trucker type wearing jeans, a dirty T-shirt that he was almost busting out of at the chest, and construction-worker boots. He had been dozing on one of two cots in the cell when we entered the room. Even though the other three cells were empty, the cop forced me over to the occupied cell, unlocked the door, and pushed me in.

"Here, I brought you a present, Jack. A pretty boy; I've already tried him out myself. Good meat, if I do say so myself." And then he laughed and said, "Oh, yeah, here are a couple of more presents." He dug into his pocket and came up with a couple of condom packets and tossed them to the trucker type.

"No, please, don't," I yelled, as the cop took first my right arm and cuffed it over the bars above my head and behind me and then my left arm to the other side, stretching me out, my back to the bars and me facing the inside of the cell and the grinning cop and the slobbering trucker, who was already busy crowning himself with one of the condoms. There was a wooden bench below me, behind my thighs.

"Gotta go make some calls Jack. Enjoy." and the cop left the cell, shoot the lock home, and started whistling as he sauntered back to the front of the facility. The trucker stood there in front of me for about a minute, a sloppy grin on his face, drinking me in.

"No, please don't . . ." I whimpered, but that was as much as I could get out, before he reached over with a big mitt grabbed hold of the collar of my T and just ripped it off my torso. Then he came into me with his beer breath and tried to kiss my lips while his was fiddling with my belt buckle and the zipper to my jeans. I turned my head, and his mouth landed in the hollow of my neck, where he bit me and then moved down to my chest and nipples, slurping and nipping. He took a couple of steps back as he pulled the jeans off my legs.

"Hot damn, Merry Christmas," he exclaimed. He pulled his T-shirt over his head, his biceps and chest muscles rippling and bulging. Even his muscles seemed to have muscles. And when he'd pulled his open jeans off, I was focused on the most impressive muscle he had. He was almost as big and thick as the dean was. He gave an unearthly scream and pushed me up the bars with his hands under my thighs and, after a couple of swallowing pumps of my cock, got his mouth applied to my asshole and slobbered that up pretty well.

I had my feet on the bench now, but he lifted my right leg off the bench and up almost to the bars with his left hand, while he was positioning his rod at my asshole and then he was in, plunging to the root. Up went my other leg, and I was "hammocked" there, my wrists cuffed to the bars behind and above me, my legs being held up and out by strong hands, my welted back rubbing up against the bars, and my butt suspended in air, as my ass, firmly skewered by his big pole, swayed in and out with his pumping motion. He took even longer than the cop had to shoot off up my ass. But when he did, he just let me collapse against the bars, pulled his shirt and pants back on, went back to his cot, turned his back to me, and soon drifted off into self-satisfied snores.

Exhausted and trying to escape the pain and this filthy cell, I forced myself into sleep in a sitting position on the bench, propped on one butt cheek to relieve the pressure on my ass. As I dozed off, my attention was arrested by that other condom packet just lying there next to the snoring trucker type, a threat of what still might be to come. I slowly came to as voices approached through the hall of the station. One of the voices sounded familiar.

"Ah, look at him," the familiar one was saying, "and did you have to string him up like that?"

"Uh, sorry, Coach. He was resisting."

"Yeah, I'll bet. I knew you'd do him, but I didn't want you to rough him up."

"Well, it wasn't all me, Coach. Someone other than me had been at him too."

"And these welts; they look like the work of a wrestler I had on my team a few years back."

A little laugh from the cop. "Yeah, you know me real well, Coach, I guess. And what I like. But he ain't none the worse for wear. I didn't do any of my black leather stuff on him. Well, not much, anyway."

Ah, it was all beginning to come together now. The cop and the dean were friends. The dean had put out a call on me—and to teach me a lesson for trying to run away from him, he had authorized a little rough action.

Seeman was standing over me inside the cell, the cop right behind him, and the trucker still snoring over on the cot.

"Ron, Ron, it's me, the dean." He was talking down at me now, but he turned to the cop.

"Let's get those cuffs off him now and get him into another room. You got any salve or something we can use on him?"

"Sure thing, Coach."

My hands were freed and I just collapsed onto the bench.

"I didn't get your name the other day, Ron," the dean was saying to me. "But Greg was useful in tracking down your roommate, who also gave us your car license number. We were afraid when you didn't show up anywhere. We didn't know what might have happened, so we put out a search call on you several days ago. Officer Hernandez here was sharp enough to recognize your car and called me to come and get you."

Yeah, Officer Hernandez was sharp all right—and so was his whip.

Hernandez came back with the salve when they got me into another room, someplace that looked like a small interrogation room, with a small beat-up wooden table and two rickety chairs. I was still naked, but Hernandez brought my underwear and pants along. My T-shirt was in shreds now.

"Here, stand up and lean over this table," Seeman ordered. I did so, and he gently applied the salve to the welts all over my body. Hernandez just stood there, watching, a little grin on his face and breathing pretty heavy. Out of the corner of my eye, I could see him rubbing his basket from time to time. Before Seeman was finished, Hernandez turned and left the room; off getting his rocks off at my expense again, no doubt.

"Okay, I think that will help," Seeman eventually said. "Put your pants back on and let's go."

"Go where?" I asked suspiciously. "I was on my way down the road and plan to be back on my way down the road."

"Well, you'll have to drive me over to the campus first," Seeman said. "I got a ride right out here from a meeting as soon as I heard you were here. I'm without wheels, so you're going to have to drive me back first."

What could I say? He had sprung me from the jail and, more important, seemed to have full power to put me back there if he so decided. So, we went out the door and to the car. As we were leaving I could see Hernandez off in a side room, slumped in a chair, his pants off, beating himself off with one hand and flicking his whip across his legs with the other.

We weren't more than a couple of miles down the road when Seeman started gently tracing the welt marks on my chest and belly with his right hand.

"Please, don't do that," I said.

"Do they still hurt?" He asked.

"They do sting a bit," I answered.

His hand went down and covered my basket.

"Hey, don't do that," I said. "Just stop, all right?"

But it wasn't all right. He was unbuckling my belt, unzipping my jeans, and running his hand into the opening. He bypassed my cock and my balls, and his big index finger slid on across my perineum and stopped at the rim of my channel.

"Stop; just stop that," I said. He got his left hand under my butt and pushed me forward on the seat, which gave him better entry to my ass with the fingers of his other hand, and enter he did with that index finger. He was moving it around, driving me crazy.

"We're going to have an accident if you don't stop that, Dean."

"Then pull over," he said huskily. "There, up ahead. There's a closed strip mall. Pull in behind that."

"No. Certainly not!"

His finger pushed farther in, my body jerked, and the car veered out of the lane.

"God, you're going to kill us!"

"Not if you do what I say. Not if you pull over where I told you to. You just don't get it, do you? This is all because you don't do what you're told to do. This is all because you ran off."

"Okay, okay. Pull that finger out and I'll pull over." He did, and I drove around and behind the closed strip mall. As soon as I'd gotten stopped, he had his hand back in my lap, this time stroking my cock, pumping me up. His mouth was on mine in a long, drawn-out kiss.

He broke away and opened his door. He was holding my right wrist in his left hand with a strong, wrestler's grip.

"Here, out of the car. This side. I don't want to have to chase you down, but I could if I had to."

I first tried to fasten my pants, but he just said, "No, you're not going to need to do that."

"Dean Seeman," I said. "Let's talk this over."

"No. You need to be educated; you need a Hard Knocks U. lesson in reality and in who matters and who doesn't. I told you to stay put on the campus, and you hid on me. We need to get this straightened out now."

"But—"

"Just take the damn seatbelt off and slide in this direction."

I did as he demanded. When he had me out of the car, he slammed the front passenger door, opened the back door, and pushed me down on the backseat. He produced a set of the cop's handcuffs from somewhere, snapped one end around my right wrist, and then pushed me down along the backseat, passing the linking chain through the seat belt two-thirds down the seat, and then snapped the other cuff on my left wrist. I was stretched out on the seat, my torso and arms inside the car, my butt on the edge of the door side of the seat, and my legs hanging out of the car.

He stripped my pants off and stepped back and pulled his own clothes off. He produced his ointment from somewhere and lathered up his cock, pumping it up to its gigantic proportions.

"God, Dean . . . Coach, don't do this. You split me last time. I'm still sore from that."

71

He took a gob of ointment and started working it into my asshole. I was lying on my left side, and he lifted my right leg up to give him an good view of my channel opening.

"Doesn't look too bad to me, sport; but I don't care if you are sore. I made you an offer the other day and you disrespected me. You accepted the offer and then you ran off. I'm going to make you another offer, and I want you to remember what happens when you disrespect my offers."

When he had me moistened up to his satisfaction and his own sheathed pole standing at magnificent attention, he slapped my butt and said, "Get out here. Get your butt out here, feet on the ground, chest on the seat." I wasn't moving fast enough for him, so he dragged me out of the car and brought my rear end up into the air.

"Stand wide," he said. "Stand as wide as you can—for your own good." I believed him and did so. He pulled my butt cheeks apart and brought his mouth to my asshole and tongued it briefly. Then he was only holding my left butt cheek, and I felt his cock at my hole. It reminded me of that cop's billy club. He took his time entering me, and when he was in all the way, he rocked me back and forth, pumping deep. I moaned and groaned and he grunted and sighed. After a few minutes, he turned me, rotating me around his embedded cock, and had me laying on my left side again, raising my right leg and side splitting me with continued deep pumps.

"One more time, Ron. Do you like this? Do you love this?"

"Yes, Dean," huff, puff.

"Coach, call me Coach. Do you accept my offer of a spot on the wrestling squad?" He took the root of his cock in his hand and rotated his rod around in my asshole, stretching it farther.

"Yes, Coach. Yes, I'd be happy to be on your team."

He rotated me yet again. This time my back was on the seat, and he was supporting my butt up in the air with both of his hands, suspending me and moving both his cock and my pelvis in a rapid, deep fuck. I got my legs and feet back in the car. My right foot was in the corner of the back window, and my left foot was on the ceiling above the passenger door.

The coach pumped and pumped and pumped.

"And how often are we going to do this, if I want?"

"Every day, Coach—every day, if you want."

"And what do you want me to do now?"

Silence. "I don't know, Coach, what do I want you to do?"

"You want me to fuck you, fuck you hard; fuck your brains out. Say it."

"Fuck me, Coach. Fuck me hard; fuck my brains out."

And he did that as best he could. He got a pillow off the floor and stuffed in under my hips, and then he just fucked me and fucked me and fucked me. His hands came over my hips. His right hand went to my cock, and he pumped me until I shot off all over his belly. His hands then traveled slowly up my torso and buried themselves in my chest hair. With a heave he pulled his rod out of my ass, ripped off the condom, and shot up my belly. Then he lowered his belly to mine, and moved it around, mingling my cum with his.

He stood up, put his clothes back on, made a clumsy attempt to push my pants back on as well, pushed me all the way into the car, slammed the door, and came around to the driver's side and got in.

"I'll drive the rest of the way. I'll drop you off at your dorm, Ron, where I want you to stay. I've asked Nate to look after you, and he's really looking forward to doing that. We'll establish a routine tomorrow. Understand?"

"Yes, Coach," I whimpered weakly from the backseat. He turned the ignition on, changed gears, and we were off, back to the campus.

CHAPTER SIX: DORM COUNCILOR CONTROL

Coach Seeman delivered me to Nate's door, ravished and still in handcuffs, which had been moved so that my arms were in front of me, and with my jeans barely covering my hips. When Nate answered the door, he was wearing only his briefs. As the dorm counselor, he had an actual one-bedroom apartment, including a small living room with kitchenette, a separate bedroom and a private bath—which made me wonder why he showered in the common bath so often. But I didn't wonder about that for very long, remembering how he had fucked me in that bathroom—and how he'd apparently had an appointment to fuck another one of the dorm residents there when he met me in the dorm showers. The communal bathroom was obviously one of his hunting grounds. Seeman hustled me into the bedroom and handcuffed me to the brass headboard at the top of one of two single beds in the room. Then he and Nate went into the other room and talked a while.

When Nate came back in, he was alone. I'd heard the door from the other room to the corridor close, so Seeman must have left.

"So, I hear you were planning to leave us—that you were found by the police a couple of miles from the campus."

I didn't answer.

"Now, what am I going to do with you? You don't seem to have gotten it. Coach Seeman has selected you as the team punch and wants you where he wants you when he wants you. Now you can adjust to that the easy way or the hard way. Understand?"

I still didn't answer.

"Okay, if that's the way you want it. Coach told me not to give it to you up the ass for a couple of days, to let you recover for a few days. But I've got to assert with you who's the boss here some way. Look at me. I said, look at me, and keep your eyes on me."

I looked up, as he stripped his briefs off and started working his meat. At first I could hardly see it, but as he pulled at it and stroked it, it started to fill out. It was a big, bulbous thing, darker than he was. And it wasn't long before he had worked it up to about six inches long and over two inches thick. Then he walked in closer to me. "Open up. I said open your mouth," and he lightly slapped me on the face. "Wider," he said, as I tried to comply with his command.

He placed one of his hands around the back of my head and said, "Keep your mouth open wide, and your head right at this position. Nothing else, just hold it there until and unless I tell you to move it." And then he inserted his dick in my mouth and face-fucked me until he was ready to come, upon which he pulled out of my mouth and came on my chest.

"There," he said, as he pulled his briefs back on and sat down beside me. "Remember that I can and will fuck you whenever and wherever and however I want. And so will Coach, and so will anyone else on the wrestling team and in our group who has a notion to take you. Like I said, Coach named you the team punch for the season. You understand what that means?"

"Yes, I think so," I managed to mutter.

"Good. And if you resist, or try to run away again, we'll make it harder on you. Understand?" He got a wet wash cloth and cleaned his cum off me, and then he took a tube of salve out of the nightstand drawer and began to rub salve over the welts on my torso.

"How long is this going to go on?" I asked. "When will it stop?"

"It will stop at the end of the wrestling season or when Coach has found someone else he fancies more than you. I doubt it will stop for some time, though. He says you're the best tail he's had in some time."

Oh. I would have to think what I could do about that.

"These welts aren't too bad. They should be gone in a few days. And in a few days, we'll give you some wrestling training. And then you can help work out the wrestling team— in more ways than one. Oh, and yes, day after tomorrow, we'll start with these, helping you to open up to your new role." He reached into the drawer and pulled out a couple of black, oblong rubber objects.

"What the hell are those?" I asked.

"Butt plugs," he said, "in progressively larger sizes. You've already been stretched a good bit, so we don't have to start with the smaller ones."

"No," I said.

"Yes. And if you resist, we'll add this," and he took out a belt with a lock that must have been something that he could attach one of the plugs to and keep it up my ass in a way that I couldn't get to it and pull it out. "It will only be for a couple hours a day."

"No. You can forget that."

"Okay, you obstinate bastard. I see we're going to have to do this the hard way all the way." He reached back into the drawer and pulled out a hefty flesh-colored rubber thing that I had little trouble identifying as a large rubber cock. He pulled my jeans off and then he lathered the dildo up well and quickly with some ointment. He moved over and sat on my left thigh to keep that leg down and grabbed my right leg with his right hand and pushed it up to my hole. My arms and hands were over my head, handcuffed to the headboard. The dildo was in his left hand, and he twirled the head of it around my asshole before he began pushing it in. I cried out and asked him to stop. In two inches, "Are you going to cooperate on the butt plugs?"

I didn't respond.

In three inches and rotated around, "Are you going to cooperate on the butt plugs? I know this hurts. I wanted to give you a couple of days, but you seem to want to refuse to accept what is what around here."

"Yes," I whimpered.

"Yes, what?"

"Yes, I'll cooperate."

In four inches, "What was that? I can't hear you?"

"Yes, yes!" I yelled. "Please stop!"

In five inches and rotated around. "You don't want me to stop, do you?"

"Yes, yes, please stop."

In six inches. "Wrong answer, Asshole. Tell me you love this."

"I love this," I managed through pants.

In six and a half inches and rotated around. "Tell me you love this and want me to do this to you every day."

"Oh, gawd!"

In seven and a half inches, rotated around, and a few in and out pumps.

"Oh, gawd! I love this and want you to do this to me every day!"

"Okay, since you love it so much." In eight inches, rotate, and pump; in eight and half inches and then some deep in and out pumping. And then he just pulled the dildo out in one swift slide and threw it over by the bathroom door.

"Now, for the next two days, you'll keep the handcuffs on, but I'll put you on a chain that will allow you to get to the john and shower. I like my guys clean, so you'll be taking quite a few showers and will keep yourself cleaned out good. Next week, if you are cooperating, you can start back to class. But you have to come back here to study, and you'll be wearing butt plugs while you are here—and when I'm not fucking you. Toward the end of next week, we'll give you some basic wrestling instruction and then we'll introduce you to the team. If Coach calls for you at any time, though, you'll hustle right on over to wherever he wants you. After a couple of weeks, you can go back to your dorm room—if you've been cooperating."

Swell, I thought.

"Oh, and one other thing; you'll be wearing a white bandanna around your neck when you go out. That way anyone in our larger group can recognize you. If anyone comes over to you, no matter where you are or what you're doing, and unties that bandanna, you are to go with him and let him do anything to you that he wants. Those are the ground rules. That's all you have to do."

Wonderful; I just rolled over and faced the wall and pretended that this all wasn't happening to me.

CHAPTER SEVEN: IT'S ALL DONE WITH MIRRORS

I stayed with Nate for the next two weeks, taking in my regular classes in the afternoon and spending most of the mornings learning the fundamentals of wrestling from Nate and Greg. We worked out in a small room off the main wrestling gym while the coach's regular "Greek wrestling" class went on in the main wrestling gym.

I thought I was getting the hang of it until I was called in for what Coach termed one of his "team punch events." Obviously, I was the punch part, because the coach's version of Greek wrestling was completely in the nude, and in this particular event the winner was permitted to do the sex act of his choice on the loser.

I didn't escape me that the deck was loaded, and I was expected to be the loser.

I was quickly pinned in my first match, with a tall, lithe guy with good moves to make up for only average strength. When he'd won, though, he let me off pretty easy. He just wanted to straddle my chest, his hands holding down my upper arms, and have me stroke his cock until it was engorged. Then he had me open my mouth and hold still and he slowly fucked my face until he came, in fairly quick order, all over my face, neck, and chest. All the time, the other wrestlers were gathered around, stroking their own cocks and, no doubt, planning what they'd do to me when it was their turn.

I didn't bother to think about what I'd do to a guy in the unlikely event that I pinned him.

Coach broke in at that point, though, saying that the wrestlers could continue their punch day wrestling with me some other time. He said he had some instruction of his own in mind for me that day and sent me to the showers. He told me to report back to him right afterward—and not bother to dress. I was soaping up in the showers, when one of the wrestlers, a big beefy oriental guy, with no hair anywhere but for the Fu Man Chu mustache he displayed with great pride, came in and walked right up to me. He took me by the hips and turned me this way and that. He fondled my cock and balls and squeezed one of my butt cheeks.

I protested, but he simply said, "I'm on the team. I got privileges."

Then, with a smile, he said, "Looking forward to my match with you, sport." He laughed and padded back through the steam and out of the shower.

When I returned to the wrestling gym, there were Coach, Gregg, and several of the other wrestlers, waiting for me, with big grins on their faces—all still naked, most with respectable hard-ons.

"Come over here," Coach said, and he led me to a strange alcove off the gym, which was shaped like half a hexagon and was completely lined with mirrors—on the walls, on the ceiling, and even on the floor. A wooden bar went all the way around at about waist height. "Like it?" Coach asked. "This is where the wrestlers and bodybuilders can come to get a good look at how various muscles are developing. We have other good uses for it too. This is going to be a sensory lesson for you. I want you and Greg to stand over there in the middle of the alcove, facing each other, hands at sides. Yes, but closer. But not too close yet."

I looked into Greg's eyes. He had that "eat you up" expression on his face. It wasn't at all unpleasant, but I felt myself trembling anyway. I was in the unknown here and had zero control.

"First, I want you to take note of yourself and Greg in all of the mirrors around you. Let your eyes see everything. Okay, now, as you are doing that, I want both you and Greg to reach out and gently explore each other with your hands. All the time, I want you to drink in what is happening by scanning your images in the mirror. See what various touches do both to what is being touched and to other areas of your body. There, that's good. Ah, I see that you're enjoying this." Greg was brushing his hands around my nipples and down to my belly, and my cock was rising in reaction.

"See, not just your cock is reacting. Look at your other muscles. Your body is coming alive to Greg's touch. See your butt muscles twitching. See your knees getting soft. And as he moves his hand to your cock, see yourself leaning into him. You want him. Your body wants him. Connect the touch sensations with the visual. See what you are doing to him with your touch. See his eyes take on a dreamy look, his mouth open and his tongue moistening his lips. Yes, see how your lips come together and open to each other, how you move into each other, nipples touching nipples, pelvis against pelvis, cock against cock. See how you both start to grind a bit. He's got his hands on your butt cheeks. Feel that, let your eyes see that, feel how the visual intensifies the pleasure of his hands squeezing your butt. Yes, you can put your hands on his as well.

"Uh, I saw you flinch. Did you see yourself flinch as Greg did whatever he did? Draw apart a bit, Greg, and let us all

86

see what caused that flinch. As yes, do you see, Ron, Greg has your cocks encased together and he's gently stroking them together. How does being able to see that enhance how it feels? Doesn't it double the pleasure?

"Now Greg is moving down your body, kissing and sucking your nipples, tonguing down your six pack, playing with your navel, kissing and tonguing down across your belly. Watch him do this from every angle, Ron. Feel his worshipping of your beautiful body. Those are your balls he's licking, Ron. Did you notice how you broadened your stance to give him access? Did you see that in the mirror? Do you realize that this means you want him? You want him to suck your balls and make love to your cock. Did you hear the sigh—your sigh— and see your hands go to the back of his head when he took your balls in his mouth?

"There, he has the head of your cock in his mouth now. Did you see as well as feel yourself throw your head back at that? Did you hear your moan? Did you see yourself burying your hands in the hair on his head, holding him to you, loving what his mouth was doing to the head of your cock? There, did you see as well as feel your cock disappear, reappear, and then disappear?

"Look at the floor mirror, right under you. That's your big cock being swallowed, disappearing in Greg's mouth. Doesn't it give you pleasure to see what you are doing to Greg and how much he wants you in him? Do you see as well as feel his hands on your butt, the finger he has at your asshole? Do you see as well as feel your cock grow even longer and thicker as it disappears and then reappears; disappears and reappears? Do you see yourself shuddering and your legs turning to jelly? Being able to both see and feel will double your pleasure, but it will also shorten your jackoff time. There, just as I said. Did you see how your body jerked and spasmed right before you shot off all over Greg's welcoming lips and face? Do you see that if he wasn't supporting you with his hands on your butt, you would have just collapsed on the floor?

"Now, Greg wants attention too. Turn around, Greg, hands on the bar, chest parallel with your butt, legs well apart. Look in the mirror, Ron. What stands out? First, that big dick swinging between his legs, right? Look in the mirrors Ron, look at Greg's dick from every angle. He was so busy working on you that he let it go a little soft again. Help him with that, Ron. You can take that big rod in your hand. Yes, like that. Milk him, Ron, and watch yourself milking him from every angle of the mirrors. And watch him loving it."

I was loving it now too. I never would have thought that arousal could be this intense. And I could see in the mirrors that all of the wrestlers standing around on the periphery were also milking themselves, or each other, and loving it.

"Now what's the other thing you notice calling to you, Ron? Yes, right, that puckered asshole. It's calling to you. Kiss it, lick it, tongue it, giving him a good rimming. And watch yourself in the mirror—and also watch how Greg is writhing from and loving your attention. Now, see, I'm going to get behind you and reach through your legs and work on your cock as well. See that in the mirror, Ron, and feel it doubly fine because you can see what I'm doing? We want you up again, because in just a few minutes, you're going to be ramming that ole eight-incher of yours up Greg's ass, and we're all going to be loving watching that in the mirrors."

I worked on Greg and Seeman worked on me for a few minutes, until Greg started to babble, "Now, now. I can't take this teasing any more. Fuck me now. Ram it up there."

"Well, do as he says," Seeman directed as he released my now-engorged cock. I stood and approached Greg's rear. I positioned my cock head against his asshole with my hand and slowly worked my way in, watching, as Coach wanted me to, from every angle in the mirror, my cock disappearing into Greg's ass. I had both of my hands on his hips now, and Gregg was pumping his own cock with his hand. Seeman was standing behind me, working up his own rod. I had to admit it; being able to watch it was twice the pleasant sensation.

I was so concentrated on working Gregg that it came as quite a surprise when I felt hands on my butt cheeks and a mouth on my asshole. I looked around wildly to see Coach's face plastered to my ass. He was good enough, though, to lather me up with some ointment before he mounted me from the back. The mirror revealed me as a sandwich, the meat between two ecstatic pieces of white bread. More than just the three of us came in near proximity of each other. The wrestlers gathered around reached climaxes, either singularly or in pairs, at about the same time.

CHAPTER EIGHT: POSSIBLE EXIT TICKET AND MARK OF THE WHITE BANDANNA

Later that afternoon I got my first glimpse of my possible ticket out of this "team punch" hell I knew was coming up again soon. I went to class, and the professor, who was also my faculty adviser, asked me to come see her in her office after her next class. When I appeared there, she wasn't alone. A young student was sitting and chatting with her. I took to him immediately. He was perhaps the most handsome youth I'd ever seen; tall and lithe, but well muscled. It was his face that attracted me immediately, however. Dark, curly hair, with a curl running down his forehead, beautiful soft hazel eyes, big full lips, and a brilliant smile, and a cleft chin and a pretty deep tan. He just exuded sensuality without putting any effort into, or, it seemed, realizing he had it. I immediately thought of Dean Seeman and what it is he liked in his choices for team punch.

"Ron, this is Ben," my professor said. "He's a freshman and is in one of my introductory classes and is looking for extra study help and a mentor. I thought you might be willing to take him on."

Take him on? And maybe lather him up and serve him up to Seeman to get out of my bondage? No problem.

Ben and I talked for a while that afternoon about his studies and his other activities. He smiled a lot and seemed to take to me right off. I ascertained that his tan came from playing a lot of tennis. That luckily was my best sport as well, so we set up a friendly match at the intramural sports center the next afternoon—during a time when I knew few others would be around the facility.

I was fairly walking on air as I left for the dorm that afternoon, seeing some prospect now of changing my circumstances. I didn't really notice at first that a car was gliding along beside me, and even when a voice called out to me to give him my white bandanna, it took me several seconds to catch onto where I was and what this request meant. I turned to see a hippy-type guy in an old Cadillac convertible riding slowly alongside me. He had a craggy face that looked somewhat familiar, except the dark sunglasses hid quite a bit. He had a light beard and mustache and long, silky dirty-blond hair that reached below his shoulders. He was wearing a T-shirt with his face and some writing on the front, and there was a guitar case in his backseat. And then it dawned on me. This was a guitarist from a local band that had gone national several years ago and still had tunes on the charts.

I stood there and looked at him, and he sat there in his car and looked me up and down, and I didn't quite know what to say.

"I see you're wearing a white bandanna, guy, and I like what I see. So, do you want to give me that bandanna to hold for a while and come around and get in and I'll give you a ride?"

"A ride?" I asked lamely.

"Yes, a ride." And then he snickered and added, "I'll even let you ride in my car." Oh, I see, and it all clicked in what I was supposed to do now. I bleakly walked around and got into his car, and he pulled away from the curb.

"Drag?" he said, as he offered what obviously was more than a cigarette to me. I declined the offer.

"Don't worry, I won't keep you long. Gotta gig myself, but I like, you know, like to get off before I go on stage. And after too, for that matter," and he gave another little laugh. I don't know how high he was already, but I kept very quiet so he could concentrate on his driving.

"Do this often?" he asked, as we drove out into the countryside?

"No. No, I don't," I answered.

"Have you done this bandanna bit ever before?"

"No. No, I haven't."

"Sweet!"

He pulled into a large county park and drove into the far end of a secluded parking lot and turned around and backed his Cadillac up to the edge of a little dell.

"Get on out, and come around to the trunk," he said, as he opened his door, got out, stripped his jeans and briefs off, and threw them in the backseat. We both walked around to the trunk of the car. He got me between him and the trunk and turned me toward him.

"Take off the shirt." I did as he asked, and he ran his hands around my torso. "Nice," he said, as he took the joint out of his mouth and offered it to me again. I declined once more.

"Oh, well, your loss." Then he unbuckled my belt, unfastened my jeans, pulled down my zipper, and took my jeans and briefs down and off my legs.

"Just a minute," I finally worked up the courage to say. "I was told this white bandanna thing was a university wrestling team arrangement. How—?"

"Coach Seeman is a good friend of mine . . . a very good friend. We do favors for each other."

Oh, of course.

He was running his hands down my flanks. "Oh my, yes; nice, very nice indeed. Go back on the trunk, please." I did so and he asked me to hold his smoldering joint and started tonguing my chest and nipples, his silky hair swishing over my torso in a not-unpleasant sensation. He worked his way down to my cock and balls and then pushed my legs up into my chest with both hands and started tonguing my asshole. After a while, he stood, and without releasing my legs, walked his pelvis into mine. His hardened, but not particularly large rod slipped into my asshole. He started a slow, almost lethargic stroking.

I couldn't help it. I moaned for him. This wasn't the rough, almost angry taking that I had suffered recently. There was no passion in it, but his cock knew where my prostate was and how to work it. And he fucked me gently, almost languidly, making me hold my breath when he was sliding deep, begging him in my mind to return to the rubbing of the prostate, which he faithfully did on the return journey. I sighed, closed my eyes, and turned my head, pretending that someone else—some young hunk, like Ted, who I had known in junior college and had secretly pined for, not really realizing it then—was making love to me.

"I'll take the joint back, if you please."

95

The monotone drone of his statement jerked me back into the present. I gave him the joint, and he puffed on that while he continued working my ass. I closed my eyes and turned my head, once more trying to grasp the scene I had been weaving, trying to reach back to the "almost ready to come" state his prostate work had brought me to.

He came inside me and then just instructed me to put my clothes back on as he walked around to the driver's side. He asked me where I had been going, and he dropped me off right at my dorm. Before I got out of the car, though, he put his hand on my arm.

"Here's your bandanna back. Best fuck I've had in this program. Thanks a lot." And then he handed me a ticket, which had a red band on the side. "Here's a ticket to my concert here Saturday night. The red band on it will get you into the party afterward. Hope to see you there." And then he just drove off and left me there on the curb.

CHAPTER NINE: MEETING MR. GARGANTUA

After dinner, Nate told me that both Coach Seeman and he had been very pleased with how I had responded that morning in the wrestling gym and that they had decided I could go back to my old dorm room with Lance.

"But first a little final-night ceremony, though. Strip and lie on the bed over there." "It's been a tough day, Nate. Couldn't we just . . . ?"

"No, we couldn't 'just.' Don't make me reassess the decision to let you go back to your dorm room. Now, you can go ahead and take that butt plug out, too." Nate stripped and came over and pushed my right leg up, bent at the knee, foot on mattress, and sat down behind me.

"Now I want you to masturbate yourself, and I want you to continue doing that until you've jacked off, no matter what else is happening." I took my cock in my hand and started stroking it.

"I think it's time you met Mr. Gargantua."

"Gargantua? What's that?"

"It's this," and Nate pulled out a long cock-shaped, dark blue dildo that had deep ribbing going around it like a barber's pole.

Oh great, I thought. But at least it didn't look too thick.

Nate lathered up my asshole with ointment, all the time watching me masturbate and telling me to continue. And then he worked the dildo into my ass. Not too bad, I thought. And then he turned Gargantua on. It was a vibrator and it revolved and sent its ribbings up and down my ass canal. This actually felt good, and it wasn't long before I jacked off for Nate. I noticed that he was jacking himself too. And then he clicked something else on Gargantua and it began to expand like a balloon, filling me and working my ass walls with those ribbings. This was something else altogether. I was loving it and hating it at the same time, wanting more and trying to escape at the same time, writhing and bucking in pleasure and pain. And then Gargantua was gone and Nate was in me instead, pumping and rocking me until he came, and just laying there on top of me as dusk turned to dark.

CHAPTER TEN: A MARINE'S GO AT A WRESTLING TEAM PUNCH DAY

My next team punch event defeat wasn't too taxing, I was getting steeled to these attacks on my body. The winner was one of those lean, mean former Marines, without an ounce of fat on a very efficient body and a shaved haircut.

Not much to brag about in the below-the-belt category, which probably is why I'd seen him hang out with one of the bantam-weight wrestlers, a willowy, but obviously strong, young man who didn't look a day older than eighteen, although he must have been at least that age to be going to this university. I'd seen them fucking on a mat in the corner of the wrestling room early one morning, and by the way the bantam-weight guy was writhing and mouthing off how good he was getting it, the Marine had found just the right fit to make up for the lack of size in the equipment department.

The Marine-type had me pinned in no time flat. Then he sat down in a crosslegged lotus position and had me sit down in his lap, facing him, my legs stretched out in front of me with his torso between them. He told me to arch back and support myself from behind with the heel of my hands, and then he let his hands roam across my torso and stroked both my cock and his until his was large enough to work with. He told me to dig my heels in and lift my pelvis a bit, which I did, and then he inserted his engorged, but not all that long or thick cock into my ass, leaned back on his own hands to give himself leverage, and fucked me with short jabs upward.

What he lacked in equipment, he made up for in stamina and the ability to reach my prostate with the bulb of his cock, as he pumped me for a good long time, and I must say I probably was enjoying this as much as he did. My enjoyment showed in the condition of my own pecker, and a short time later, the Marine's little bantam-weight type, probably in an act of jealousy, came over and settled between the Marine's torso and mine.

My cock was running up the cleavage of his pert little butt, and he put a hand back there to simulate a channel for me to fuck, so I dry-fucked him. I had already figured out he and the Marine were a matched set because of his size and the size of the Marine's penis, so I didn't press the point about trying to enter the tyke myself. There wasn't anything small about my equipment. The Marine and his lover went into a session of kissy-face and mutual nipple nibble, and I figured they had forgotten me altogether when I felt the Marine withdraw from me and start skewering the bantam-weighter.

I slid right on out from underneath them after I'd shoot off up the bantam-weighter's back, and they gave no evidence of noticing I'd gone. It almost looked like they were wrestling until the little guy's torso flopped back and away from the Marine's lap, and I could see the root of the Marine's cock vibrating at the rim of the bantam-weighter's hole. The bantam-weighter obviously thought he was being taken well.

CHAPTER ELEVEN: SUCKED BY A BLACK LIMOUSINE; TURN FROM THE WOMAN'S VIEW

I had several white bandanna encounters that week in which all a stranger needed to do to get submissive sex from me was to ask for my bandanna. Coach Seeman certainly had a lot of friends he was exchanging favors with. I wondered what he was getting from these guys. None of these encounters were as strange as the one I had while I was on my way to play tennis with Ben the first time. I was strolling along, racket case under my arm, when a big black limousine with smoked windows rolled up beside me, the driver's window rolled down, and a big black bullet-headed chauffeur pointed out my white bandanna to me and told me to follow his car into the far end of an almost-deserted parking lot. I followed him. The car had pulled up by an unusually high curb, and when I got there and walked around to stand on the curb where the limo was between me and the busy street off a ways in the distance, the rear window of the car came down, and a voice issued from the dark depths of the rear seat.

"Lean in just here and put your hands on the roof of the car. Keep your eyes on the street over there." I did so. The curb was high enough that my pelvis was at the level of the window. I felt my tennis shorts and jock strap being pulled to below my butt cheeks. One thin hand went around to a butt cheek and the other one went up under my tennis shirt and rested on my belly. My cock was being worked by a mouth— and rather expertly worked, I might add. There I was, trying to look nonchalantly over the roof of the car, while pedestrians passed by in the near distance, looking at me, full of curiosity about the nifty limo over here, while I was getting a very interesting and expert blow job and ball wash and nibble. When I had come, which was efficiently swallowed, and had been licked clean, my shorts and jock were snapped back into place, I was told to back off from the limo, the back window rolled back up, and limo moved majestically across the parking lot and back into traffic.

There were other peculiar white bandanna encounters, of course. One day not long after my limo blow job I was accosted by a woman who knew both my name and to use the white bandanna to get me into her car, which was not a hard car to want to get into; it was a big white Bentley. The woman looked nice and rich too. She was on the edge of being a matron, but money had kept her on the well-maintained side. She was in great shape and would be very attractive in candlelight. And I certainly was ready for a change of pace.

It took us more than five minutes just to drive from her front gate up to her big house on a hill. As we walked up to the door, it opened and it all came together for me. Standing in the door, welcoming us in was one of the school's prize wrestlers, Samir, who we called Sam. A tall, rangy son of the Levant, Sam was a cream and coffee-colored hottie, with strong legs and a long, lean torso topped with broad shoulders and tremendous biceps and pecs. It appeared that in this world, though, he was Mrs. Rich's butler. He was wearing a tight tux shirt with big cuffs and cufflinks and a bow tie, topping a pair of silk, skin-hugging black pants that fit every contour of his body from his waist down to his calves and then flared out to hems topping a nice pair of patent-leather pumps. And it obviously was Sam who had gotten me hooked up with his mistress, although my mind was working double time to try to figure out just what form of mistress she was to him. Sam was giving us a big welcoming grin.

Mrs. Rich led me to a guest room, waved at the closet, and told me to strip and put on the items I found in the closet. She assured me that there were several of each item in there and I should be able to find everything in a size that would fit me. After I changed, she said, I should look over on the dressing table for further instructions. She told me where she wanted me to go after I'd changed and left me in the room alone. I stripped down to my briefs before checking the closet out, enjoying the uncertainty of what I'd find behind that door.

Right before she'd left, Mrs. Rich leaned down to where I was sitting and breathed in my ear, "You make this entertaining, Sweetie, and there will be a two-hundred-dollar tip in it for you."

Wow. A two-hundred-dollar tip for a good performance. I'd been fucked four ways from Sunday in the last couple of weeks. There wasn't much left for me to lose. None of these other bandanna guys had given me a tip like this, although the Cadillac hippy had given me tickets to something I knew little about. "Sure thing, Missus," I answered back. And, what the hell, this was so bizarre is was a bit fun. I'd give her a good performance.

When I appeared in Mrs. Rich's bedroom nearly thirty minutes later, I was wearing a silky scarlet slip, a blonde wig, and a heavy layer of bright red lipstick. Under the slip, I was wearing a black lacy bra and what I'd call black lacy breakaway bikini panties, meaning that they tied at the sides with string and could be easily pulled off. I also was wearing a thin garter belt around my belly, which held up black, fishnet stockings. On my feet were strapped black stiletto heels, which had been a little difficult to walk down the hall in. I must say that this getup somewhat amused me, and I was game to see where this would lead.

I met my double when I entered Mrs. Rich's bedroom. Mrs. Rich herself was identically attired and was stretched out on a chaise lounge facing her gigantic bed. She looked fine in this light, but I wondered if I perhaps didn't look a little bit better. She looked me up and down and told me in no uncertain terms that she liked what she saw. Then she asked me to go over and perch at the foot of the bed, and, after I'd done that, she rang a buzzer and Samir appeared. She simply told Samir to come over and sit beside me on the bed and to make love to me, as if I was a woman, until she told him to stop. She pointed out that there was a tube of lubricant on the coverlet beside me, which he could use, but that in all other ways I was to be a woman to him and that I was to consider myself to be a woman to him, a woman who loved him and would deny him nothing.

Hookay.

Samir sat down on the bed beside me and gently turned my face to him. He gave me a gentle kiss, and I opened to him in the way I felt a woman in love would do. He seemed surprised at my response, at my willingness to play this game, and his kiss turned passionate. He put his right arm around me at my hip and bunched up the silk slip in his fist. His left hand went to my belly, which he caressed and then let his hand drift up to my neck and then down my cleavage and to my breasts. I covered his right fist with one of my hands and raised my other hand to his cheek. And I sighed for him as I thought a woman would sigh when he touched my breast. This seemed to send a little thrill through him, and I wondered if he was begging to forget that I wasn't really a woman. From across the room, I could see that Mrs. Rich was enjoying this immensely.

Samir had bunched up my silk slip on one side to the point that the hem had come up to his hand. He moved the other hand down to my other hip, and we broke our kiss while he pulled the silk slip up and off me. His lips went to the hollow of my neck, and he went into a lingering kiss of my pulsating artery there. His right hand was spread on my lower belly, his little finger just under the waistband of my bikini briefs. His left hand was frantically exploring my breasts above the bra, feeling me and squeezing me. He seemed to be into this exploration even though I didn't have big breasts. Of course, I didn't have little breasts either; my pecs were very well defined, and he could certainly feel my taut nipples through the flimsy material of the bra.

Thinking that this is what a woman would do, I took his hand and moved it under my bra. He flinched in pleasure at this, and I heard Mrs. Rich laugh with pleasure as well. I slowly unbuttoned his shirt and pulled the tail out of his pants. He released his hands while I pulled his shirt off his back, but then he returned them to where they had been, but now his right hand was even farther down on my lower belly. It was interesting that when I pulled his shirt away, his black bow tie and his cuffs remained. Mrs. Rich had decked him out as a Chippendale stud. And he would have fit in that line up just fine; a magnificent chest and biceps and long abs tapering down to a flat belly. His chest was heaving slightly now, as if he was having trouble controlling both his breath and his sexual appetite. He was like a lithe tiger, trying to pace himself, prolonging the kill, even though he was already loaded to pounce. And I could tell he was already loaded by the tenting in his crotch area.

I reached behind me and undid the snaps of my bra, stripped it off and threw it to the side, and then I arched my back backwards, supporting myself on my hands, my long blonde hair streaming down my back, my "breasts" open to him.

"Suck them. Suck my tits," I murmured, slightly amused by all of this, but already thinking ahead to Samir fucking me, which wasn't all that unpleasant an idea now.

With a groan, he responded immediately, burying his face in my chest, going after my nipples with his lips, enjoying me just as if I were a big-breasted woman. To help the illusion, I sighed and moaned and shuddered just as if he had found my

111

sexual switch and now I would not deny him anything as long as he carried through with ravishing me. And, truth be known, his work on my nipples was turning me on. He left that, bringing his lips back up to mine and devouring me. His bare chest was rubbing against my bare chest, and the electricity of this contact was surging between us.

I moved my right hand to his tented crotch and let him know I was interested in what he had and how big and thick it already was—and I could feel that he had a big pair of balls to go along with the package.

"Are you going to stuff all of this in me, you big stud?" I whispered.

"God, you're turning me on," he whispered back. "You really want it, don't you?"

"Oh sweet heaven," we both heard the woman murmur with a breathy voice from across the room.

Samir moved his left hand to on top of my package as well and just held and appreciated my engorging cock, while I moved on to freeing his.

With a thrill, I discovered that the front of his pants were some sort of codpiece, which I could unsnap and pull away, leaving his pants on but exposing his cock and balls. A slit seemed to run even farther, I assumed to permit access to his asshole as well if that was what was wanted. I began stroking his cock but lost leverage when His lips went back to my nipples and then started down my sternum.

Time for the woman to take control, though. With a laugh I pulled away from him and sank down in front of him, between his legs, pushing them out, and wrapping a hand around the root of his cock.

"Let me make it ready for me, Baby," I whispered.

"Oh, God," he repeated. "I'm going to fuck you silly," he added through clenched teeth.

Then he was gasping and groaning as I slowly took the cock in between my ruby-red lips, giving him a woman's suck, the most intimate of a woman's service to a man. And Samir let me service him, first leaning down over me and hefting and manipulating my "breasts" with both his hands and then, eventually, as I was bringing him to new levels of ecstasy, arching his back backward, supporting the weight of his torso on his hands and rolling his head and panting and heaving his chest, slowly giving all control over to me and concentrating his pleasure on those ruby-red lips giving his cock and balls suck.

Mrs. Rich's view of all this were parted black-silk-covered legs, between which kneeled a bare-torsoed figure with blonde hair cascading down its back, and bubble butt cheeks barely covered by black lace panties, gathered up into the valley of butt cleavage, and a black garter belt holding up black mesh stockings covering strong legs and ending in black stiletto heels pointed at Mrs. Rich. Above the bowed and bobbing blonde head, arms could be seen running up a man's heaving torso, with fingers digging into his bulging chest, ending in the underside of a man's chin. The man was burbling to himself back and forth and emitting small animal sounds of pleasure.

But then with a shudder and a loud animal sound, the tiger came alive and moved to regain control. Samir's torso came up, and his hands came down to my waist and pulled me away from him. He stood and brought me up as well. He turned both of us around and laid me down on my back on the bed. His hands went to my panties, which he pulled off me, snapping the strings. The proof I wasn't a woman was obvious. I was somewhat amused that I was as hard as he was and was both longer and thicker than he was. Samir didn't seem quite as amused, though. He went for the tub of lubricant, got a big gob and went straight for my ass. Not to lose control, I got a gob too and worked on his cock while he was working on my ass.

"I was going to be gentle," he hissed at me, outside of earshot of the woman. "But you tease. I'm going to pound you."

"Fuck me, fuck me hard, you big stud," I cried out as I arched my back. My mind was on the two-hundred-dollar tip in the offing. Not all of it, though. I was thinking of the measure my hand had taken of his cock. He was no Coach. I could handle this.

Mrs. Rich's view was of a man standing between the legs of a reclining woman in black mesh stockings, He was

114

finger fucking her, opening her up, and the woman was arching her back and moaning and voicing pleasure and in being finger fucked and opened up (just as I was doing) and stroking the man's cock, keeping him hard and interested. The only visual illusion was that Samir was lathering up my asshole rather than a cunt.

Samir pushed me back on the bed with a thrust to my sternum, obviously wanting complete control, but I slid my butt toward him, maintaining a grip on his cock. I wishboned out my legs, bringing my high-heeled feet up to dig into the edge of the bed, and it was I who guided his cock to my hole and brought him into me until reaching the point where my sphincter took over and drew him up my ass.

Then, with a laugh, I just relinquished control and let him pump me. His hands came down onto my chest and worked it as if he was kneading big tits. For Mrs. Rich's benefit, I screamed and yelled in ecstasy and put on a show with those stocking covered legs, holding them up and out briefly, and then wrapping them around above Samir's bouncing butt as if I was drawing him into me as far as possible (which is what I was doing) and then just swinging them wildly in the air as if he was splitting and ravishing me (which he certainly was trying to do).

"Stop!" Mrs. Rich commanded, and both Samir and I stopped in mid thrust. Samir turned and sat on the bed beside me as Mrs. Rich rose off her chaise lounge and ambled over to us. Samir was trying hard not to show how worked up and angry he was that she hadn't let him pound the stuffing out of me.

"I can't let you finish with Ron here, Samir. I have no idea how long it will take you to recover and the two of you were so marvelous that I'm simply a fright. If I don't get some right now, I think I'm going to melt into my shoes. Be a dear, Ron. You go over and sit on the chaise for a while now." Still panting from the exertion but mildly amused, I did as she directed. Thereupon, Mrs. Rich plopped down in the spot I'd vacated.

"Now, Samir, Baby. I want you to do exactly the same things to me that you did to Ron. And I'm so impressed by Ron's performance that I'm going to do exactly the same things to you."

Samir turned and hissed a, "Later," at me as I passed him on my way to the chaise. I sashayed my butt at him, knowing I'd have to face him on the wrestling mat someday soon—but, for the first time, looking forward to losing to someone in the Punch Day wrestling matches.

And, so, they went through the scene again, but this time, with a real woman. As far as I could tell, Samir and I had done just as well as Samir and Mrs. Rich were doing.

When Samir got to the point of finger fucking Mrs. Rich, she grabbed his hand and laughed. "The same as with Ron, Samir. I'm not interested in having your children." So, he

116

took a gob of lubricant and went for her ass instead of her cunt.

At the same point where Mrs. Rich had stopped the scene between Samir and me, she stopped the scene between Samir and her. A "Stop!" rang out, and Samir, on the edge of shooting off, responded to her command immediately. I wondered both at his control and what control Mrs. Rich must have over him to keep him in check like this.

"I don't want to have your child, Samir. But I think I wouldn't mind having Ron's child. He's better looking and better built than you are, don't you think, even as presentable as you are? And he certainly has a longer and thicker cock. I think he can go where you couldn't. Please be a lamb and pick up your things and be ready to take Ron home when I call."

A sullen Samir grabbed up his shirt and codpiece and stalked to the door and out of the room. Mrs. Rich beckoned to me and said, "Now, once more from the beginning, shall we? You can be the man this time." And so we did, and I must say, Mrs. Rich could have taught me a thing of two about blowing a man, and I was never so happy to be tooling around in a woman's vagina once more.

When I withdrew from Mrs. Rich and turned to leave, she produced two hundred-dollar bills and tucked them into my garter belt. With this brief act, she turned me into no more than a paid prostitute, even lower in status than Samir, who had been perfunctorily dismissed as inferior in equipment to me.

When I finished, had showered and cleaned the makeup off my face, and was dressed, Samir was waiting at the door to drive me home. He hadn't bothered to put his shirt and codpiece back on. He was coldly polite. We got in the Bentley and floated back down toward the gate. However, in the wooded area before reaching the gate, Samir stopped the car and turned it off.

"Now, it's my turn to invoke the power of the white bandanna."

"Look, Samir," I said. "I just did what I was told, and I didn't take any part in trying to embarrass you." I was tired from the two sessions. I was looking forward to Samir, but I thought it would come later, on the wrestling mat.

"That doesn't matter. None of that matters. I got you up here; I engineered your visit up here because I wanted to do you myself. And I want you on my own terms, not through any little play directing by that woman up there—and then made into a tease by you. Even if I'd been able to finish with you up there, we'd be here and I'd be invoking the power of the white bandanna. Now strip."

While, with resignation, I was doing so, Samir opened the moon roof and pushed the button that lowered the front passenger seat until it was almost flat. He told me to get on my knees on the passenger seat, facing the windshield and then he

118

stood on the passenger floor, facing me, his chest rising out of the moon roof.

"Now blow me. And make it slow and interesting and complete." It only took me a couple of minutes to bring him to climax, which was understandable because of the two times Mrs. Rich had denied him climax up at the house.

"Well, that was disappointing," he said. "Very pleasant for as long as it lasted, but disappointing all the same. OK, I'm going to play with you until I recover, and then we'll see what we see."

He came back into the car compartment, pushed me down the flat passenger seat and hovered over me, toying with me. It didn't help matters that I had shot off twice myself before his cock had gotten hard enough to perform. Then he just stretched out on top of me, and fucked me and fucked me, taking me from the side, with one of my legs stretched up to the moon roof; and then from the back, with me kneeling on the seat and him standing over me with an arm around my belly and pulling me up to him like I was a barbell in an exercise, burying himself farther in me with each lift; and then from the front, with one of my feet wedged in the top corner of the window sill and the other dug into the corner of the moon roof for leverage, and then, at last, once more from the side, both of us scooting toward the backseat with the force of his thrusts. It may have taken him some time to recover, but recover he had, as he shot off into me twice and then up the

119

small of my back twice more in torrents of hot, angry Arab cum.

CHAPTER TWELVE: SUBORNING A SUBSTITUTE; MEXICAN STANDOFF, OR NOT

The exhaustion of and loss of strength from the previous day's unexpected sexual encounters may have accounted for my tennis match the next day, but it's just as likely that Ben was just a much better tennis player than I was. He agreed to let me try to recoup the loss and set up another match for two days hence. As I had hoped, we were the only ones in the intramural gym shower room when we went in to shower and change.

I quickly showered while Ben lingered in getting undressed. He hit the showers after me, and I soon figured out why. I was sitting there on the bench in front of the lockers when I got a side view of him at a corner shower head. I swallowed my breath and almost my tongue. It wasn't enough that the young man was an Apollo, but he was horse hung as well. A good eight or nine inches and it was standing very much at attention now. He looked quite sexy with that tan line that had been established with a very skimpy bikini brief. The contrast between dark tan and light skin was almost as if he was wearing briefs but transparent ones that framed the viewing of his full package perfectly. As I watched, he masturbated himself. It was all I could do to keep myself from masturbating as well. And I was still telling myself that I wasn't queer, that I just had gotten in with the wrong bunch and couldn't extricate myself.

He shot off, and his cock started to deflate, but he must have noticed me watching him, because he came over, a towel wrapped around his middle and red from embarrassment.

"I'm so sorry you saw that, Ron," he stammered out. "It isn't what you think. I've got this medical condition, you see. I usually have a doctor who takes care of it, but I haven't found one here yet. It's this condition where I build up semen too fast and have to be milked regularly, or I get a hard-on that won't go away. It can be very painful."

"Yes, I guess so." Especially when you're hung like a horse, I wanted to add. "But, no worries, Ben. I know all about that condition."

"You do?"

"Yes, of course. I worked as a physical trainer and physician's assistant at my former college. And I worked for a doctor who had patients like that he had to treat. I know all about it." I was finding it quite easy to tell the big lies. I continued, "In fact, if you haven't found a doctor by day after tomorrow, I think I can help you with that."

"You can? Okay, that would be great. Because this hard-on has been driving me crazy"

I hope I know someone else who it will drive crazy too, Ben, I thought to myself. Boy, these freshmen can really be naïve.

That night Lance tried to put his moves on me, but I wasn't having any of it and he just went back to his bed and noisily jacked off, covers off, hoping I was watching. I couldn't help myself; I was.

Surprising everyone, I didn't lose the next team punch event. I didn't win, either, but, hey, a draw was better than getting fucked. The guy was a surly Hispanic—Mexican I was told later—with an attitude, not that there was anything wrong with being a Hispanic, but a surly dude of any ethnicity was to be avoided at all costs. He was pumped up with steroids or something that made him look like a professional wrestler, and he had a whole display of tattooing that covered one whole half of him. It came down from his skull—he had half of his head shaved, and the hair on the other half drooped down into his eyes. The tattoo descended his neck, covered the left half of his torso and his left arm, and descended down his left leg after making a detour around the root of his cock. It was a rather intriguing design, but I wasn't all that interested in getting a better look at it. He had rings in his eyebrow, in his lip, in his right nipple, in his navel, and, most shocking of all, in the foreskin of his penis, which was a pretty respectable size and uncut. He looked like he'd just stepped out of a gang-banger comic book, and I was mighty glad I didn't lose my match to him.

For some reason, I was able to keep him from pinning me and I just wore him— and me—out until the coach called the match. The gang-banger was furious, gave me an evil "I'll get even" look, and marched off.

I was feeling on cloud nine when I went off to my tennis match with Ben, and I almost won a set from him. When we got to the showers, I saw that his condition was bothering him again—kinda bothered me too in a different way.

"You found a doctor for that yet?" I asked, my heart in my throat.

"No. They don't exactly advertise it in the Yellow Pages, and I'm afraid I'm too embarrassed to ask around."

Then, after a pause, "But did you say you might be able to help?"

"Yes, I possibly could. It would be a little irregular and I don't want you to get any ideas, but I do know and have performed the procedure. I could try helping you until you can get a regular doctor. I wouldn't want this to sour anything between us in our study arrangement, of course. I only offer it because I know how painful that is, and how hard it is to talk about and to get help for."

"Well, I don't know," Ben said.

"Of course, it sometimes helps if someone else does the masturbating, you know."

"Excuse me?"

"Well, it is a sex condition. Your body obviously wants more than you can get. The doctors I worked with told me that the body's production can be fooled into thinking you're getting enough action and just produce less if the stimulation comes from someone else. Again, this is just medical stuff. I wouldn't want you to think otherwise."

"Well, I guess I could try that; if you'd be willing, of course. I wouldn't want to embarrass you."

"Well, I'm game if you are. Get on back in the shower." I left my shorts on just so he wouldn't be spooked, and went into the shower with him. Standing close beside him, while the water spilled over the both of us, I took that gigantic tool in my right hand, and slowly jerked him off to ejaculation.

I made sure not to make any other gesture that took the action beyond what he could convince himself was clinical and in his best interest.

He thanked me profusely afterward and chastely turned away from me in the locker room to dress, although I sensed that there was something else in his eyes when he looked at me that hadn't been there before this milking job. We set another tennis date; we already were meeting regularly for study.

"Well, I do hope that helped, Ben, and that you're able to find a doctor soon. If it doesn't, of course, I could always give you a prostate procedure after our next tennis game. The doctors I worked for always combined it with a body massage so the patient was relaxed. There are private massage rooms here no one uses, and I'm sure we could do it here without fanfare."

"Well, I don't know. I certainly don't want to impose. We'll see when the next tennis match comes around."

That evening when I was going back to the dorm from the library, I heard this motorcycle rev up as it came down the street, and it slid up beside me. I looked around, and, Oh, Lord, it was the gang-banger. All decked out as a nasty biker. Big Harley or some such, leather pants, leather boots, leather captain's hat, and leather vest, but no shirt.

"Now, look, I'm not interested in any trouble," I said, as I moved away from him a bit.

"Hey, Hot Shot," he said, "I see you're wearing a white bandanna. Give it to me and hop on the cycle behind me."

What could I do? I climbed onto the bike behind him. I tried my best to keep from touching him with my pelvis, as we roared off, but I had to wrap my arms around his bare, steely midsection.

We didn't motor for long before he pulled up to a large corrugated garage building. He had a device in a pouch hanging off his cycle to zap at the door to make it open, and then he zapped it closed again when we drove into the building. He ran his cycle right up to a clearing in the middle, under some gymnastic arm rings, stopped it, and kicked down the kick stand as he hopped off. He went over to the side and picked up a pile of leather material and tossed it at me.

"Here. Strip and put these on." It dawned on me that he must have come out specifically looking for me. I tried arguing with him, but he kept dangling the white bandanna at me and repeating that it was a ticket to whatever he wanted to do. Did I want him to tell the coach I wasn't cooperative?

I stripped. My new costume was composed of a leather harness crisscrossing my chest, leather chaps, leather boots, and thick leather wristbands lined with fleece.

"Come over here and get back on the cycle, turn to the back, your back on the handlebars." When I'd done that, he quickly attached a long chain to my right wristband, threw the chain through one of the gymnast rings overhead and attached the other end to my left wristband. There was some give in the chain, but I couldn't bring my hands and arms to in front of me. He then attached shorter chains through rings in the ankles of my boots to something in the wheel of the motorcycle on either side.

I was doing quite a bit of objecting at this point, so he plopped a rubber plug into my mouth, which had straps that permitted it to be tied off behind my head. I was fully at his mercy now, and he wasn't in a merciful mood. He stripped his own pants off then, and stood there in his leather vest and boots—and that busy tattoo and all those metal rings piercing his body. He already had quite a hard-on.

He took out a camera and took "memory" shots of me astride his cycle and in restraints. I showed him I didn't like that, but he just laughed. He brought out a tube of ointment and started lathering up my ass, while pumping my cock with his other hand. When he had me all lathered up and pumped up, he took out the camera again and took some "hard-on" shots of me. Then he set up video cameras on pods that zeroed in on the bike and me from three different directions, turned up the lights on the "set," and came back to the bike, He threw his leg over the bike and was sitting on the seat, facing me. The video cameras were running, as he ran his hands over my torso and thighs and stroked his own cock until it was hard enough for him. Then he tilted my ass up with his hands on my butt cheeks and entered me. He was in fine shape and was very vocal for the cameras.

"Nice tight ass, and nice tits, Hot Shot. Gonna fuck you until your eyeballs are swimming in cum. There, you want me. I'm in and you're pulling me farther in. Can't get enough of me, can you? Been eyeing me for weeks, haven't you? Ah, made you moan, made you flinch, made you pant. You haven't had a man until you've had me, have you?" I could feel the ring on his penis head dragging across my prostate and jangling against my ass walls. I was much too angry about the whole setup, though, to consider whether this was an added sensual benefit or not.

And he pumped and pumped and pumped, showing off for the cameras. When he was about to blow, he withdrew, stood up, and sent his cum flying all over my chest and belly, no doubt also for the cameras. He got up and switched off the cameras. He came back with a damp cloth and wiped me down, and then he wiped himself down. He did this all in silence. I was ready to just get out of there. But he wasn't ready yet. He kept moving around the garage, working himself up for what I'd learn was the finale, recharging his load. He came over to me and wrapped a leather ring, with studs around the base of my cock, ensuring that I would remain hard for the cameras when I got hard again. Then I saw him encase his own cock in some sort of sheath and strap something around his head and over his mouth that looked like big lips. He moved his lips up and down, making sure that the device moved with him. Then he turned the video cameras back on and came back to the bike, once more throwing his leg over the saddle and facing me. It wasn't long before I learned what his new lips were.

The lip device was charged somehow, with batteries or something. It emitted a low-level electrical charge that registered at just above the tingle stage. It did have an electrical zap feel to it, but only just at the threshold of being painful.

The gang-banger removed his vest—for the cameras—and both his unseen audience and I were mesmerized by the rippling of his muscles as he started to kiss me with those lips from my neck to my underarms and biceps, across my chest to my nipples, and down my sternum to my belly, navel, pubic region, and cock and balls, sending slight electric shocks into me wherever it touched. Pleasure mixed with pain, causing me to jerk slightly for the cameras with each touch of the lips. Electric pinpricks to my tender inner thighs, on my butt cheeks, across my perineum, on my balls, and firmly applied to the rim of my asshole. I jerked and jumped with each touch.

Then I found out about that sheath covering his cock. He tilted up my ass with hands under my butt. His cock slid into me again, and I found that the sheath was electrified too. But the voltage here was higher. He was manually operating the jolts somehow, applying the first one as he slid over my prostate, causing my whole torso to lift off the bike handles in pain and sending me into spasms that had barely subsided when the second jolt hit me, all along the ass canal some five inches down; another half inch and another jolt. His lips went to my nipples and held onto them, one after another, sending electrical shocks into me there, and below he was six and half inches in and another, stronger, more prolonged jolt. It lifted my torso off the bike and took him with me. He wrapped his arms around my waist and rode with me, giving the muffled shout through his electrified lips, "Whooeee! Ride 'em, Cowboy!"

Seven inches in and a jolt that made me pass out.

They found me on the dorm steps later that evening, fully clothed, my white bandanna wrapped around my neck, and my books beside me. Thinking I had just passed out from too much drink, they hauled me in and tossed me in my bed.

The next day I had a conference with Coach Seeman, who quite agreed with me that there were limits to this arrangement and who assured me that the photos and videotapes would be found and destroyed. I never saw or heard of the gang-banger again. I didn't really care if he was found and destroyed as well.

CHAPTER THIRTEEN: SENSUAL MASSAGE TIMES TWO

My next team punch event day was more memorable for being the day of the double massage than for my losing a wrestling match and getting fucked. I lost the match, of course. This time to Greg, who was perverse enough to make me swing both my arms and legs over the parallel bars and then got on a bench under me and fucked me first from the front, my ass tipped up and then from the back, my ass tipped back, and then back again. The trick for him was in making the transition, which he did several times, without dislodging his prick from my ass. The trick for me was to take the pressure and weight on my arms and biceps for the thirty-minute performance. The other weightlifters seemed to be quite entertained by this.

The first of the double massages came after my tennis match with Ben, in which I won a set but lost the match. He hadn't found a doctor yet and was rock hard solid again and had been so for a day, so we both agreed that the prostate procedure was the next logical step to relief. I really didn't have to convince him to do this; he was in that much distress and he seemed to trust my intentions completely.

After our showers, I pulled on gym shorts and he wrapped a towel around himself and we went looking for the most remote massage room we could find. I had him on his back on the table in short order. We dispensed with the towel, as we agreed that the procedure would include the prostate procedure, with me masturbating him, and there wasn't much privacy involved in that. I rubbed him down real well from head to toe, not touching his cock, and had him turn over. He groaned as his hard-on came between him and the table and I told him it would be okay for him to raise his pelvis a bit to give him more room there. I rubbed him down on this side and then announced that he seemed to be relaxed enough for me to proceed if he still wanted to do this. He said he did.

So, taking a large gob of ointment in my fingers, I began rubbing it into his asshole, moving a finger in a bit farther with each pass. I hoped that this all seemed medical enough. When his hole had opened and his sphincter had pulled my index finger in and positioned the pad of the finger on the prostate, Ben began to moan and pant. He looked so beautiful there, stretched out on the table, that I had the urge to rise up there and just mount him. His butt was raised and inviting. But I resisted. Ben was not for me. Ben was my freedom. He "oohed" and "ahhed" as I gently rubbed and put pressure on his prostate. He also began to slowly grind the table with his pelvis, a sight that I enjoyed immensely.

"Okay, turn over," I said. "I'm going to try to keep my finger in position." He did and I did. His huge cock went straight up in the air. I encased it in my other hand and stroked it as I continued to milk his prostate. Cum was bubbling up and out of his dick. I felt pressure on my elbow, and a looked around to see that Ben was gripping my arm. Whether he realized it or not, he was giving me that "fuck me, fuck me now" look with his beautiful hazel eyes. It broke my heart, but I didn't know if he realized what he now wanted from me and he was not for me. If I'd taken him, I don't know that I'd ever be able to deny, even to myself, what I was becoming or that I'd be able to turn him over to the coach to substitute for me in getting the education I was getting.

His pelvis lifted into the air as he ejaculated straight up—several times. He certainly did have a lot of extra sperm to give. I had lost position with my finger, but when his pelvis had come back to the table, I just kept milking and sperm just kept bubbling up for several more minutes. All I could think was that Coach Seeman was going to love this.

* * * *

Later that afternoon Professor Hollings cornered me for the second massage of the day. We were passing each other in the hall at the university, when his hand shot out and he pulled me over to the side.

"You haven't been back to see me," he hissed.

"I'm sorry, Professor, I've really been busy."

"My place in an hour," he shot back.

"I'm sorry, but I have to—"

"Give me that white bandanna." I handed it over to him. Of course he'd been one of the group, one of Coach Seeman's special friends. "My place in an hour; I'm going to fuck you, and then you're going to give me a nice massage."

He answered the door in his robe.

"The room where I take my massages is through there. Through the kitchen. But first. Take everything off. Take it off right here." I stripped, wondering if he'd gone off his nut or something.

"Here. Follow me to the kitchen." We'd gotten half way through the kitchen, when he turned on me and said. "Up on the counter; hop up on that counter."

Well, Hokay. Up I perched on the kitchen counter, between the sink and the stove. The counter was some sort of granite; cold on the butt cheeks. He slipped his robe off and was naked. He already had a half hard-on. I watched him cross to the refrigerator and return with a tub of butter. To my surprise, He dipped his hand in the butter, came up with a big glob and started smearing in all over my chest and belly.

Hey, I thought—and think I said it as well—but he pushed me back on the counter and his lips went to my chest, while his hand kept coming up with gobs of butter which he smeared onto my cock and balls and then into my asshole as his lips followed, down my body, playing cleanup. But his lips didn't follow into my asshole. He slid his cock in there, without removing the butter and gave me a butter fuck. It was all a little kicky and more fun than what some others were doing to me.

He pointed to a bathroom with a shower between the kitchen and his workout room. When I emerged, all clean again, he was laying face up on his massage table. I gave him a massage, both front and back and he toyed with my cock whenever he could get to it. So, as a fringe benefit, when I was done with his back, I whipped out that old tub of butter and started buttering up his ass.

"Hey, wait," he said, "that isn't part of my plan."

"No, but it's part of mine," I said, as I got up over him on the table, I was down on my right knee beside his thigh on one side, and up on my left foot on the other to maintain

137

leverage and aid thrust. I ran my arm under his belly and lifted him up to me and entered him. He was disagreeable at first, but after the first five minutes, he was panting and groaning, and sighing, and moaning, and asking for more. And I gave him more. I gave him a whole lot more. I gave him more than seven inches. It seemed the only logical thing to do. He'd been the one who started this whole story.

I felt so good about having fought back at my circumstances that evening that I let Lance, of my own free will, go to sleep with his long cock up my ass and my ass folded into his pelvis. And I think I was as content with and comforted by this as he was.

CHAPTER FOURTEEN: SERVING THE BAND

I still felt better about the possibilities of taking control the next evening, which may be why I took that ticket the doped up rocker had given me and attended his concert. His band really was quite good. He had a large crowd in the university's soccer stadium, and it was even filmed for national sale as a video. The rocker who had fucked me had a great, raspy, character-laden voice and he played a mean guitar. I was also impressed with his backup singer, a statuesque brunette in a halter top and flowing crinkly skirt. She played a hand harp as well as sang. The drummer was an evening's entertainment himself. Stripped to the waist, and sweating from the exertion, he was a massive Jamaican, with flowing dreadlocks that flew all around him as he made love to his drums. The spots were on him more than on anyone else that evening.

Caught up in the euphoria of the concert, I decided to see what my special red-banded ticket would get me. I really wanted to see that brunette up close. My wish on that was granted, because when I was ushered back to the rocker's dressing room, she and he were in a lip lock and fondle exercise over on one of a pair of couches that faced each other in an alcove. The room was thick with the smoke from various drugs, and a small crowd was freely handing around a foaming drink in big plastic cups. The rocker saw me and waved me over. I sat across from him and the striking brunette. They offered me a joint, but I turned it down just as I had the other day. I did take a drink and downed it quickly, though, which likely was a mistake.

I think I had been slipped a Mickey of some sort, because it wasn't long before I got groggy and my connection with all that was going on around me kept going in and out. I started to disappear, while the brunette appeared wrapped up in whatever conversation I could muster to avoid telling her I was here because her colleague had had me for a snack a few days earlier. She must have fancied me herself, because after my first blackout, I found her on my sofa, sticking her tongue in my ear and playing with my chest and belly. My shirt had disappeared somewhere. I didn't stay aware long, and the next time I put in an appearance, the brunette was still there, toying with me, but my rocker friend was now on the other side of me.

My pants were down around my ankles, and the rocker and brunette were kissing each other across my body and each of them had a hand on my hardened cock. Surprisingly enough the room still seemed to be full of boisterous people. Next I was aware; the brunette was sitting astride my lap with my cock up her cunt. Her skirt still flowed around us, but her big tits were flapping against my chest and her long hair was whipping my face. The music, which had a good beat, was louder than the crowd now, and, good musician that she was, she was keeping great time with the beat in her bucking in my lap. As far as I remembered, the rocker was puffing a weed and playing with both the brunette's tits and my nipples as they bounced against each other.

In the next scene that I was allowed to witness, the brunette was still fucking herself with my hard cock, but the rocker was under me. I was sitting in his lap, my butt nuzzled into his pelvis and his hard penis up my ass.

I don't know how all of that came to a climax, but it must have satisfied them, because they gave me a ride home in the rocker's Cadillac convertible. For the brief time I was awake, I found that I sort of was sitting sideways on the backseat of the Caddie, at least the back part of my bare butt in the brunette's lap. She was sitting in regular fashion on the

141

passenger side of the backseat and must have been sitting on a cushion, because we were sitting pretty high up out of the seat. I was leaning back against the side of the car, and she seemed to be playing my torso like her harp and spending a lot of time on my still-hard—or hard once again, as far as I knew—cock and balls while I weighed and squeezed her big jugs.

My left leg was draped up onto the back of the seat and my right leg was draped over into the front seat and rested on the rocker's shoulder. He was driving while trying to suck my toes. What was most interesting, though, was that the Jamaican drummer was kneeling between my spread legs. He had a club of a dick disappearing in my asshole and reappearing from my asshole in a heavy rock rhythm, while he drummed a beat set to his pumping with his fingers on my belly. His beautiful, glistening chocolate chest was heaving and rocking back and forth, and his head was spinning, keeping his long dreadlocks twirling in the air in time with the thrusts of his pelvis into my ass. It was really a wonderful sight for the short time I was aware of it. I was sort of sorry I missed most of the performance—and especially the climax.

CHAPTER FIFTEEN: NOT ENTIRELY A LOSS

The Oriental mountain with the Fu Man Chu had at me at the next wrestling team punch event. As an incentive for me to resist defeat, the wrestler had been permitted to equip himself with a cock sheath that had all sorts of rubber knobs and scratchy things running up and down it. I didn't really need an incentive to try to win against this nearly hairless giant of a man, but the strength and training just weren't there, and after he had slammed me on my back while on his knees by wrapping one arm around my thighs and lifting them up, while pushing me down on the floor with a big paw on my sternum, he just walked right on into me on his knees and pushed that prickly, knobby-covered pole up my ass. I did some yelling and pawing of the air, but as an encore, he swiveled me on that enhanced skewer, rolled onto his back, and wrapped a beefy arm around my chest.

"Lift yourself up on your feet," he whispered in my ear, "or I'm going to hurt you."

Hurt me? What did he think he was doing now? But I didn't like the prospect of him thinking he could do worse, so I got my feet on the ground and lifted my pelvis, and so did he underneath me, which gave him room and leverage to pump that collection of knobs and prickles in and out in my ass canal for a good fifteen minutes before he spewed his load. The wrestlers seemed to enjoy it, especially when someone brought out a big mirror that gave them a good view of that decorated sheath coming out and plunging in in rapid rhythm. As Fu Man Chu was shooting his load, Nate added to the festivities by going at his ass with Mr. Gargantua, while I paid him back for violating the "completely naked" rule by wrapping my arms around him and helping to hold him in place.

CHAPTER SIXTEEN: AN AFTERNOON OF DOUBLES

At my next tennis match with Ben, he allowed as how he wasn't in nearly the same painfully hard condition that he had been when we'd done the prostate procedure, but he did show a bit too much eagerness to repeat the massage that day if I thought it was advisable. I wanted him at full staff for presentation to the coach, so I asked him if he could hold off until our next practice match, to which Ben almost wistfully replied that he thought he might, but he'd probably be in pretty bad shape then. I thought that bad shape, under the circumstances, was all relative and that this probably could be ideal, if I could just hang in there myself for a couple of more days.

That proved a bit of a trial to accomplish though. Nate white bandannaed me the next day, taking me out to a construction site on a large new home. I thought it would be Nate I'd have to endure, but when we got there, there were three grinning, strong-looking construction workers waiting for us.

"These guys are working on Coach Seeman's new house, Ron. He thinks they are doing a marvelous job, so he's lending you to them as a little reward."

Very generous of him, I thought bitterly. I wonder how he can afford to be so generous.

They led me into what would be the basement, and two of them stripped down to just their hard hats, their tool belts, and their boots, as the third one slowly stripped me down, feeling me up as clothing items were shed and sucking me off as the other two construction workers and Nate watched. I was just standing there leaning against what was going to be a load-bearing pole. The one working on me was actually the youngest and best looking by far. He was stripped down to just cutoff jeans, and I didn't particularly mind him giving me a slow and easy blow job. The other two construction workers were licking their lips and fondling and stroking themselves as they watched the younger one going down on me.

When I had shot my load, one of the other construction workers came over and took me roughly by the hand and led me over to a makeshift apparatus that the other one was pulling together. He had taken two low sawhorses and slapped a pine board between them. The first construction worker pushed me over on my belly on top of the board and started shoving his big, engorged dick at my asshole, finally managing to push in and slowly plow me to his root.

The other construction worker came around in front of me, grabbed my hair with his hand, shoved his dick in my mouth and fucked my face. Meanwhile the worker who had blown me, came back under the sawhorse and began licking my balls and cock again. After a good ten minutes of this, the two workers who were stuffing me changed positions. The one behind me withdrew from me and pushed me over to a picnic table that was being used as a work bench. It had two bench seats that weren't connected to the table. The one I had been blowing now came at me from the front, pushing me down on the table on my back, wishboning my legs, and fucked me from the front. The one who originally had been boning me got up on his knees on the bench seat at my head, held my shoulders down on the table, and took his turn face fucking me. Just before my mouth got turned and stuffed I looked over and saw that Nate was allowing the better-looking construction worker to plow his ass at the sawhorse position. Well, I thought, at least Seeman was being generous with all of his assets.

* * * *

My next team punch event was really unfair, but Coach Seeman was looking forward to something special, and the Pratt twins apparently didn't go anywhere or do anything separately. I was faced with two identical accomplished wrestlers. Of course it was no contest, and the gym roared with delight and everyone was cheering and groping each other as the twins, as their reward for winning such a one-sided battle, shared me.

First one went down on the floor with his legs stretched out in front of him, and then the other one helped push me down into the first one's lap, facing him, my ass slowly opening up to his average-sized cock, not yet ready for the onslaught. This twin wanted to kiss me and lick and nibble at my nipples. The first one's rod was only an inch in when the second one scooted under me from the back. Now the twins were essentially sitting facing each other close, the legs of the first one stretched alongside the hips of the second one and the legs of the second one extending over the thighs of the first and wrapping around his butt. I was between them, my legs now on top of those of the second twin. And the second twin's cock had joined that of the first one at my asshole, and as I was stretching and opening up, I was descending on two cocks. Luckily they both were of average size. Both twins were

148

frenzied at sharing me and running their cocks together up my ass canal, and I was a little excited too. As Twin Number 1 continued to kiss and nibble at me in front, Twin Number 2 wrapped his arms around me and found my cock and balls and gave them attention. He also kissed and nibbled at my shoulder blades and neck.

Upon an almost imperceptible command after they were both rooted in me, Twin Number 1 lowered his back onto the floor, and, with his hands squeezing my butt cheeks got his feet up onto the ground, raising me with his thighs and tipping my butt into the air. Twin Number 1 then came up on one knee and got the foot of the other leg onto the ground and, with this new leverage, power fucked me with his cock, at the same time creating friction with his twin's cock that sent the three of us into exclamations of ecstasy, panting, and grunts and that sent the audience into cheers. The three of us came in near succession, although I'm happy to say that I outdistanced both of the twins in this category.

As I untangled myself and hobbled for the showers, Coach Seeman patted me on the butt and told me this had been my best performance yet.

CHAPTER SEVENTEEN: MEETING MR. RIGHT AT THE SWIMMING POOL

Coach Seeman had told all of the wrestlers that they could come over and use his swimming pool at any time, and I was so sore and strung out later that afternoon that I took him up on the offer. I knew there was a wrestling meet during that time and figured that Seeman and the real wrestlers would be busy with that and that I'd have the pool to myself.

I did, in fact, have the pool to myself for almost the first hour I was there. I laid out on a lounge and got heated up for a while and then I went into the pool and swam laps. I probably swam a good many, as I was trying to numb myself to my circumstances. When I came up out of the pool and was toweling myself off, though, I noticed I no longer was alone.

Andreas, one of the more intriguing members of the wrestling team was stretched out on the other lounge, which was right beside the one I had been using. I say intriguing, because he always seemed to be missing or in the background during my team punch ordeals. I knew he was queer—or at least bi—because I had seen him having hot sex with Greg in the wrestling gym showers once, but he had never hit on me yet. Which, given the choice, was a little disappointing, because he was one of the hottest of the wrestlers.

He was Greek and had the tanned Mediterranean coloring and the good bone and muscle structure and easy flowing movements of that ethnic type. He had curly black hair, a handsome face, with flashing white teeth, and an easy smile. There was also curly black hair on his forearms, and his calves, in his arm pits, and across his chest and down the front of his body, but I wouldn't necessarily say he was particularly hairy. Maybe he would turn that way in his later years. I knew from watching him and Greg going at it that he had a very nice package, and that was evident now as well with a view to his skimpy sock swim suit as he stretched out on the chaise close to where I now sat. With a sigh, I stretched out and closed my eyes, trying both to pretend I was alone and not to follow up on my natural attraction to Andreas.

Silence for a while and then, "Hi, I'm Andreas. I've been told your name is Ron." "Yes," I answered, trying to be both polite and distant.

"I'm sorry you're having such rough time at wrestling."

"Yes, well . . . Thanks." I kept it at that for a moment, but then I said, "I thought there was a serious wrestling meet today and that you'd all be at that."

"The other team couldn't muster up enough wrestlers in my weight class, so I wasn't needed."

"Oh."

"Well, as I said, I'm sorry you are being used by the wrestlers as you are. I wouldn't do that to anyone who objected."

"I'll bet no one has ever objected if you asked." I responded. Now why did I say that?

He laughed. "Well, I don't keep track, so I don't know if that's true."

"So, you don't join in . . . with the other wrestlers . . . because you don't like sex that much?" I was pretty sure that wasn't true based on what I've seen.

"Oh, no. I like sex all right. In fact, I like it just fine. I'm Greek. Really from Greece. We seem an uptight culture, but we're really pretty free with that sort of stuff underneath The Grecco form of wrestling, for instance. What Coach Seeman has bastardized here. That's really done in the buff, and I grew up doing that. No, I've grown up getting sex freely and whenever I could give it."

"So you're what, straight, bi, gay?"

"Oh, I guess you could call me bi. I was fucking girls and lonely housewives when I was fifteen. Guess I've always been able to do that when I wanted. But I'll admit that I fooled around with other wrestlers pretty early too. And when I went into the army, it was the accepted thing to do. At first, we'd go down to the back fence in the evening when we felt the pressure and we'd get blow jobs from the queers who gathered there to feed on handsome young and fit soldiers. Then some of us would go on to having sex with each other during guard duty in remote areas, just to escape the boredom and because they did their best to keep us away from the neighborhood goods and we were heavy with testosterone."

"Sounds like Greek boys are really randy."

"Yes. I'd fuck another boy, or a man, or a girl, or a middle-aged woman . . . or a sheep."

"God, a sheep?" That got me looking over him all bug eyed.

"No, not really," he laughed. "Some Greek boys will do that. But I've never done it. It goes back to why I told you I was sorry for what you're going through. I like the sex, but only if the choice of it is mutual. I don't like to force myself on anyone, and I've never had to do that."

154

"So, you haven't joined in with me because either you feel sorry for me or I repulse you."

"Oh no, neither of those. I'm mad at what they do to guys like you, and you certainly don't repulse me; quite the opposite."

Silence for a few minutes.

"And you. You don't enjoy it, do you?" Andreas asked.

Silence for a few minutes.

"Well, sometimes I do, I guess. It's increasingly getting to where sometimes it gives me pleasure as well. I had sort of a fun role-playing game at a rich woman's house recently, but that just turned into more of the same, being taken by force. The sad thing is that I wouldn't have minded being fucked by the guy if he'd asked me nicely. But all of this wrestling punch day and white bandanna game stuff still scares me and makes me mad most of the time. Being used like that."

"So, it's not the act. It's the force and being used?"

Silence for a few minutes.

"Yeah, I guess that might be it."

"And do I . . . do I repulse you?"

A rather weak "No." And then stronger. "No. You are one of the most desirable of the wrestlers. I . . . I saw you with Greg. I am drawn to Greg, too, but he pushes at me too much for me to really enjoy it. But seeing you and Greg. I almost . . ."

"I think I like you better than I like Greg. I bet we could—"

155

Silence for a few seconds. "Yes, I think we might too."

"If I come over there, would I be forcing myself on you?"

A few seconds of silence.

"No, don't think so. I think I might like that . . . if we went slowly. I have a pretty sore ass, as you can imagine."

I watched as Andreas fluidly rose from his lounge. He stood beside mine for a minute while he untied the strings to his sock suit and let it fall to the ground. I experienced a thrill and a big intake of breath, as I saw his magnificent body in complete nakedness once more. He leaned over and pulled my Speedo down and off my legs and then he stretched himself on top of me and we kissed and enjoyed the sensation of our bodies touching. Our hands in a firm grip, with arms stretching above our heads, touching all along their stretch. Our lips on lips and tongues playing with tongues; our chest and nipples rubbing; our hearts thumping in rhythm; our bellies touching, both panting a bit, our pelvises and cocks touching, entwining, increasingly grinding; our thighs rubbing; our toes touching and running up each other's thighs. Our entwining became more hurried and we writhed against each other, enjoyed our bodies chafing against each other.

We turned so I was on top, and then we were on our sides, facing each other, and after that he was on top again. We panted and moaned and sighed as our cocks engaged as swords and we dry fucked each other up our bellies or between our thighs. Neither of us was moving to take control, but we were both aggressive and submissive at the same time. We decided to release our hands almost simultaneously—neither of us would have been able to say whose idea that was—and our hands joined the exploration, heightening our sexual tension and our frenzied play.

But it was more than the exploration that was causing us to heat up. We were being fried by the sun. I, because I had the most sensitive skin and he was naturally tanned from life in the Mediterranean, was the first to break, declaring that I was being cooked and had to go into the pool to cool off. His dive was right behind mine, just as neat as mine, and we both stroked to the end of the pool and immediately went into another lip lock, our fingers more aggressively exploring each other under the water.

Andreas hauled me up to where I was sitting on the side of the pool, my legs in the water, and he gave me a slow, expert, complete blow job. When he finished, I lay back on the cooking tiles, oblivious to the heat, and raised my arms across my face, blocking out the sun, completely enjoying the moment. He ran his hand up my hips and waist and held them there at my sides. He still held my cock in his mouth, waiting for it to subside, not wishing to abandon it until I was soft once more.

I found myself calling out to him, almost in a whisper, "Fuck me, Andreas. I want you to fuck me?"

"What is that you said?" he asked in surprise.

"Fuck me. It's my choice. I can't feel liberated from all this until I've made the choice freely, myself. I want to make that choice with you. Fuck me. Just do it gently, please. I'm still sore inside."

He rose up to me and entered me and fucked me, gently at least at first, but then passion swept us both up and the sex became very hot—but mutually satisfying. He hadn't been pumping me for long before he noticed that I was stretched out on the hot tile surrounding the swimming pool. He slowly slid me back into the swimming pool and we discovered that sex was much more interesting and whole new positions were possible when the partners are immersed in water.

CHAPTER EIGHTEEN: PULLING THE SWITCH

The next day was my next tennis date with Ben. As I had thought and hoped for, after we'd played and I'd beaten him for the first time, I learned that he was in bad condition again and needed help. We both took showers, and he started back for the massage room, but I stopped him, telling him I had found a better place for him to get relief. We hurriedly both put gym shorts and T-shirts on, and I walked him across campus . . . to Dean Seeman's office. I'd already called ahead and told the dean I was going to try to bring him a treat along about now, so I knew he'd be in his office.

No one was in the outer room when we arrived, but I could hear the low, happy whistling from inside Seeman's office, and before Ben could ask what was happening, I propelled him into the room and beside the dean, who as usual in this office on days he had held wrestling practice, was wearing baggy gym shorts and an athletic T-shirt with deep arm and chest V's.

As he had done with me, as soon as Ben got near enough to snag, Seeman was turning and examining and pinching and prodding him without paying any attention to Ben's questions and yelping. When he pulled down Ben's shorts to take a look, he let out a yelp of his own.

"Hot Damn! Will you look at that monster cock? Just look at that monster hard-on. It seems a sin to give someone as good looking as this a cock to die for too. Will you look at that hard-on?"

"And it stays hard most of the time," I helpfully interjected over Ben's shoulder.

"Well, I gotta get some of this right now," Seeman declared. "Here, Ron, you know the stance. Get him in a good position for me."

Vividly remembering my first day here, I remembered to get behind Ben, between him and the desk and, first, strip off my own T-shirt, and then push the front of my shorts and briefs down, and then strip off Ben's T-shirt from the back and put an arm lock on him that raised his arms over his head.

160

Then I leaned back into the desk and brought him back with me, remembering, as Gregg had done, to get my dick running up the small of his back. I also somewhat belatedly remembered to wrap my calves around Ben's so he was essentially held in place until Seeman wanted to move them. Ben was moaning and whining and neither Seeman nor I paid a bit of attention to him.

As he had done with me, Seeman stripped Ben's shorts and briefs off—and I had to free Ben's calves momentarily so he could do that—and then he was focused on that nice, big, juicy cock. Seeman's hands and mouth went to Ben's cock and balls and he ravaged the young man. Wanting to change the scene I was familiar with and assuming no one would notice in this onslaught, I got my cock up under Ben and began an entry. I found that Seeman's finger was there ahead of me and he had already found Ben's prostate, but he didn't seem to mind the company of my slowly ascending cock. When I encountered Seeman's finger work, I felt slightly better for Ben. He was getting what he needed; milked. And Seeman was to find what I found. That even after Ben had shot off in several fountain exhibitions, the semen just kept on bubbling out for several minutes more.

Ben seemed to be taking this pretty well now. He had gotten dreamy eyed, and he had gotten his balls off and alleviated the pain from that, and, oddly, I got the impression that he didn't mind all that much having my cock up him. And it would probably have been a good enough educational experience for him then if Seeman hadn't, like he had done to me under the same circumstances, taken it to another level when Ben had been totally milked and his cock had begun to soften.

Seeman reached down for Ben's legs. I felt this was happening and released Ben's calves from my leg hold. Lifting and wishboning the youngster's legs out, Seeman rolled his chair in toward the desk, and I felt his cock at Ben's hole. I tipped Ben back farther to move my cock to the back of his hole, and Seeman was pushing his monster cock in and the young man was screaming bloody murder once more. The feel of Seeman's sausage plowing up under my cock was too much for me, and I shoot my load. Seeman, who had obviously just loved working with Ben's cock, wasn't far behind me in ejaculating. So, at least Ben was saved any pumping action, which is more than I can say for my first double fuck. Ben just lolled there between the two of us in semiconsciousness, and I thought it was now or never in selling this deal.

"So, what do you think, Coach? You think Ben here could be a wrestler?"

"On my team he could. Yes, certainly."

"How about the next team punch? Look at that cock, Coach. Look at that face and body. Wouldn't he be a great next team punch?"

"Why yes, yes he would, now that you mention it."

Coach sat there for several minutes, Ben still skewered by both of us, and traced his fingers over Ben's magnificent, if temporary bruised and wounded, body; across the fine lines of his face. "Yes, yes. I think you might be right, Ron. If, of course you didn't leave the group."

"No, no," I said somewhat wistfully, "I think I've crossed some sort of line here today. I guess I wouldn't be leaving the group now."

"Well, you go on home now, Ron. Ben here and I have some discussing to do."

I pulled out of Ben and put my T-shirt and shorts back on and headed for the door. When I got there, I turned to take another look. What I saw made me stop to look longer, the memory of my own encounter here, just a couple of months ago flashing into my brain. Seeman had Ben flat on his back on the desk. He was holding his right leg up and out, and holding the youngster down on the table with a strong mitt applied to his belly. Ben was squirming, but not getting anywhere. Seeman had his big dick buried in Ben's ass still, and he was starting to pump him.

"Great definition in these muscles," Seeman was saying. "Athletic. You could be a wrestler. You should come out for wrestling. We have a tight little wrestling group. Your tight ass would be a good addition. What do you say? Come out for wrestling next semester. I could give you some one-on-one coaching."

Ben whimpered something that I couldn't hear.

"What was that you said?" Seeman asked. He took both of Ben's legs in his hands and positioned the young man's feet on the edge of the desk, and Ben had the good sense to keep them there, as it gave him leverage to accommodate Seeman's pounding dick. Seeman then moved his hands onto Ben's chest, digging into his pecs, squeezing his nipples hard.

"Yes, coach. Yes, I'd like that."

"We could do this about every day," Seeman said, as he took the root of his cock in his hand and rotated it inside Ben's ass. Ben let out a frightened little moan.

"Would you like that? Would you like me in you, fucking your brains out nearly every day?" Seeman now had his hands on Ben's butt cheeks, squeezing them. He was pumping Ben hard now.

"Yes, Coach. Oh please—"

I turned and walked away. Before I left the building, though, I ripped the white bandanna off my neck and dropped it on Greg's desk. I think it was fair to say that this part of my education was complete now. I could have fooled myself into rationalizing that Ben was getting what he needed, frequent milking to alleviate that hard cock condition he had. But I wouldn't be fooling anyone but myself if I took comfort in that. During the past several weeks, I had been asking myself how people like Professor Hollings and Dean Seeman came to

be the way they were. Now I knew. I had gotten that
education. I was on that road now myself.

ABOUT THE AUTHOR

Habu is one of the pen names of a former supersonic spy jet pilot, intelligence agent, male model, movie actor, and diplomat. A wild youth in South East Asia was spent enjoying whatever sexual opportunities came his way, and much of his gay male writing is about recalling incidents from those days and inventing ones he'd perhaps have liked to experience. He now leads a very quiet and ordinary happily married family life.

An American, he is a published mainstream novelist and short story writer under another name and in another dimension of his life. He has written or cowritten (with Sabb) over 500 published short stories and nearly 100 published erotica e-books, primarily of gay fiction but also memoir, straight fiction and ménage fiction. His hand and creative writing can be seen in stories and books by habu, sr71plt, Dirk Hessian, Shabbu, and Stephen Kessel—among unrevealed others that might surprise readers. The fictionalized GM memoir *Flying High, Diving Deep* is loosely based on his life experiences. He can be found at the adults only gay male site BarbarianSpy, which he shares with Sabb and Dirk Hessian.

Our authors always like to receive feedback, and appreciate it when readers post reviews at Goodreads, Amazon, and other sites.

BarbarianSpy

FOR LITERARY HEAT

Not all books listed below may currently be on release.

BOOKS BY DIRK HESSIAN

Xtreme Erotica

The King's Men

Shores of Tripoli

Prophecy of Noto

General Erotica

Constantinople

The Beautiful Way

Blue and Gray

Colonel's Treasure

Beginning of Time

Labyrinth

BOOKS BY HABU

Gay Erotica

Memoir Faction

Flying High, Diving Deep

Xtreme Erotica

Second Coming

Dark Angel Sounding

General Erotica

My Neighbour's Spa

Finding Amnad

Beyond the Beaded Curtain

Hard Knocks U

Man's Man

Trip Money

Vortex

Clint Folsom Mysteries Compendium Volume 1

Clint Folsom Mysteries Compendium Volume 2

Grab Bag 1

Grab Bag 2

Grab Bag 3

The Indian Doctor
Sailorboy
Home to Fire Island
The Sporting Life
Platres Conclave
Fetish Galore!
Choke Hold
Literary Gay Erotica
Cairo Surrender
The Handyman
Homeward Bound
Journey to Mirage
Menage Erotica
13 Ways for Halloween
Luther
The Indian Prince
BOOKS BY SHABBU
Yap, Yap
Dirty Pool
Operation Black Jade
Cigars!
Angel in the Barn
Gayly Complicated
Despoiling David
The Tree of Idleness
I Met a Man
The Interview
Rough Road to Happiness
BOOKS BY SABB
The Legend of Holleystone Grange
Surprise Encounters
She is He
Wrong Man
Loyal to his King
Barbarian Tales - Book One - Traveler's Tales
Barbarian Tales - Book Two - Journeys Begin
Barbarian Tales - Book Three - The Inheritance
Barbarian Tales - Book Four - Road to Persepolis

~